THE SILKEN CORD OF LOVE

THE SILKEN CORD OF LOVE

Vicki Page

Chivers Press • G.K. Hall & Co.
Bath, England   Thorndike, Maine USA

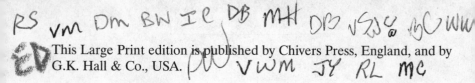

This Large Print edition is published by Chivers Press, England, and by G.K. Hall & Co., USA.

Published in 1998 in the U.K. by arrangement with the author's estate.

Published in 1998 in the U.S. by arrangement with Chivers Press, Ltd.

U.K. Hardcover ISBN 0-7540-3186-1 (Chivers Large Print)
U.K. Softcover ISBN 0-7540-3187-X (Camden Large Print)
U.S. Softcover ISBN 0-7838- 8387-0 (Nightingale Series Edition)

The text of this Large Print edition is unabridged.
Other aspects of the book may vary from the original edition.

Set in 16 pt. New Times Roman.

Printed in Great Britain on acid-free paper.

British Library Cataloguing in Publication Data available

Library of Congress Cataloging-in-Publication Data

Page, Vicki.
    The silken cord of love / by Vicki Page.
        p. cm.
    ISBN 0-7838-8387-0 (alk. paper)
    1. Large type books.   I. Title.
    [PR6066.A355S55   1998]
    823' .914–dc21   97-32595

CHAPTER ONE

The telephone bell rang stridently in the night silence of Rayne Stenning's small flat. She stirred restlessly in her sleep then, with a sudden flash of panic, she sat up in bed, groping for the receiver in the darkness.

'Hello!' she said.

There was a brief pause as she waited for the caller to speak. The luminous hands on her clock pointed to ten to two. Who could be ringing her at this hour? It was probably a wrong number.

'Hello! Is that you, Rayne?'

The sound of her cousin's voice startled her into immediate wakefulness. Valerie Palmer would not be phoning at such an unearthly hour unless there was something wrong.

'Yes. What's the matter, Val? Are you all right?'

She felt her fingers tighten on the receiver as she waited for her cousin to speak. The brief seconds seemed to lengthen into an eternity as a host of questions flooded into her mind. Past experience had taught her that Valerie was sadly lacking in discernment and occasionally even common sense. Although she was twenty-two and two years Rayne's senior, it had always been accepted that Rayne was the practical one, the one who managed to extricate her from the many and nefarious scrapes into which her impulsive, headstrong behaviour had sometimes led her. What could it be now?

The silence weighed heavily and Rayne felt the cold fingers of premonition lightly touch the nape of her neck. She reached out with her free hand, switching on the bedside lamp. A pool of light surrounded the bed, reflecting on her tousled golden hair like a nimbus. Her wide grey eyes contained a puzzled expression; she bit her lower lip with even, white teeth as impatience mounted within her.

'Val? Are you still there?'

No longer could Rayne bear the oppressive quiet of the telephone line.

'Yes ... Yes, of course I'm all right...' Valerie's voice held a tremulous uncertainty which did little to reassure Rayne or to quell the rising tide of mingled curiosity and anxiety which gripped her.

'You don't sound all right ... and why are you ringing me at this hour if everything is okay?'

'Rayne, I need your help. I—Oh, please don't be cross with me. You were the only person I could think of who would care about me ... who I could turn to for help.'

The mute appeal in Valerie's words met a responding chord within Rayne. The two girls had always been bound close by the striking similarity in their looks even if not in their characters. Their mothers had been twin sisters and, as the two girls had each inherited the fairness of the maternal side of their families, the likeness between them was remarkable. Both orphaned by a holiday plane crash while their parents were travelling en route to Kenya while they were in the safe keeping of their grandmother, their shared loss had helped to bind the two girls with a sisterly link. For longer than she could remember Rayne, despite being the younger, had felt herself responsible for her cousin.

'Why do you need my help? What's the matter?'

'I can't tell you over the telephone.'

Rayne sighed, although accustomed to Valerie's illogical approach to problems it was not easy to be patient when she had been so harshly dragged from a blissful state of sleep. A mutinous expression lit for a moment on her mouth above the faintly obstinate chin but she made a deliberate attempt to quell the irritation which was the effect her cousin so frequently aroused within her.

'If you can't tell me over the telephone, Val, I'm wondering why you chose to ring me in the middle of the night.' She controlled her voice carefully, silently deciding she would have to get herself some warm milk before she settled herself back to sleep after this weird conversation.

'You're cross with me . . . I can tell it . . .'

There sounded a small cry which could

3

almost have been a sob. Rayne tensed, wide awake now all her attention was given to her cousin. She was not usually so quick to pick up the nuances of exasperation which she provoked.

'I'm not cross, Valerie, but how can I help you if you won't tell me what's wrong?' she demanded.

'I want you to catch the first flight you can and meet me out here, Rayne. Will you do that for me?'

The words sent wave after wave of shock stirring through Rayne.

'But where *are* you . . .? You haven't even told me that . . .!'

'Lugano.'

'*Lugano . . .!*' repeated Rayne, amazement in her voice.

'Yes. It's in Switzerland . . . on the Swiss-Italian border.'

'I'm well aware where Lugano is situated, Val. What I'm not clear about is what *you're* doing there! I thought you were supposed to be taking a few days' holiday in Bournemouth.'

'It's a long story. I can't explain now. I'll tell you all about it when you get here. Oh, do please come soon, Rayne. I need you.'

Rayne swallowed hard, trying to marshal her emotions into a semblance of order. As a freelance illustrator she supposed she could arrange to take a few days off even at such short notice, but the wisdom of allowing

Valerie to believe she would drop everything to chase about the globe on her cousin's merest whim was another matter altogether. But there was in Valerie's tones a note which Rayne could not put her finger on, a tone which alerted her deeper instincts in an inexplicable manner.

'Please, Rayne! Will you come?'

The simple question dropped into the silence between them, scattering Rayne's hurried attempts to decide what she should do.

'I suppose I could join you for a few days but—'

'Thank heavens!' The relief in Val's voice was unmistakable.

'—but it can only be for a few days,' went on Rayne, warningly. 'I've some illustrations to complete for *Ladies World & Home* by the week after next so I mustn't be away for long.'

'Just a few days, Rayne. That's all it will take.'

'All what will take?' Once again those frissons of presentiment rested on Rayne before she made a deliberate attempt to shrug the feelings off.

'I've told you. I'll explain when you arrive. How soon will you be able to leave London?'

'As soon as I can arrange a flight, Val. Where are you staying?'

'I'm at the Hotel Bon Accord overlooking the lake.'

'I'll telephone you when I've arranged a seat

5

and know my arrival time.'

'No—no . . . Don't do that . . . I—I'm out such a lot. Just—just *come* to me, Rayne . . . As soon as you can . . . Please . . .!'

Even as Rayne opened her mouth to speak, a bewildered frown drawing her brow together, she heard the gentle click of the receiver being replaced on the rest at the other end of the line. She could not understand Valerie's secrecy nor the unfamiliar note which sounded in her voice. A frightened note.

Rayne felt a shiver of an echoing fear stir within her. There had been a deliberate evasion on Valerie's part when Rayne had told her she would telephone. But why . . .? The question beat insistently at Rayne.

Dawn streaked the sky with pearly light before Rayne fell into a restless doze. She dreamed that Valerie was being pursued by a gigantic tidal wave and knew that no power on earth could possibly rescue her from the crashing wall of water.

Rayne dragged herself from the troubled sleep feeling totally unrefreshed by it. Her eyes were gritty, hot and stinging and she was aware of a threatening headache. For a few seconds as she sought to pull herself together she wondered if she had dreamed about Valerie's telephone call with its desperate cry for help. As full consciousness returned, though, she knew that it had really taken place; she knew also that she must make her arrangements to fly out to Switzerland as soon as possible. All her instincts told her that Valerie would not have phoned her in the middle of the night unless each minute counted.

There was much to be done and, anxious not to waste time, Rayne got up and showered swiftly. She dressed in a businesslike navy-blue trouser suit to carry her through the next few hours which would be filled with interviews at the offices of the magazines for whom she was preparing illustrations and then a visit to the travel agency to book a flight. Mentally she ran through the list of arrangements she must make and details not to be overlooked but, at the back of her thoughts, she could still feel the vague sense of apprehension gripping her.

Her plans went smoothly. Rayne was not in the habit of asking for extra time on her commissions and the editors whom she met were all co-operative.

The last call she made was to the travel agent and she was lucky enough to book on a flight the next day. Within a few hours she would be on her way to join her cousin and, in spite of her previous doubts, Rayne felt the more pleasurable tremors of anticipation now beginning to replace that earlier sense of misgiving.

It would be nice to have a few days in Switzerland. There was probably no place in the whole world which seemed such a far remove from the material problems of day-to-

7

day living . . . and the more Rayne reflected on that surprise telephone call from Valerie last night the more she was inclined to consider it in the light of a prank . . . a ploy to lure her—Rayne—out to join her cousin for a few days' relaxation. She smiled to herself ruefully. She had clearly let herself be used as a pawn by Valerie—and not for the first time! she added. But, meanwhile, she must concentrate on packing a few garments and closing up the flat while she took a well-earned break.

There was little time for rumination. There was much to occupy her attention and, after the near-sleepless night she had endured the night before, she was eager to get an early night so that she might be refreshed for her journey the next day.

As soon as she went to bed Rayne fell into a deep slumber, untroubled by any dreams. She had no idea how long the telephone bell had been ringing when it finally disturbed her. Bemused with sleep she reached out a hand and lifted the receiver from the rest. She really would give Valerie a piece of her mind for this inconsideration, she silently resolved, still struggling to gather her senses together.

'Hello!' she said, her voice still bleary with sleep. 'What do you want, Valerie? Why can't you ring at a more conventional hour?'

But the male voice which answered did not belong to Valerie. The shock awoke Rayne into full consciousness, each nerve in her body alert

8

to this unknown caller and the reason for the call.

'Miss Stenning? Is that Rayne Stenning speaking?' The caller's voice was pleasant, courteous. Rayne thought she detected a slight accent.

'Yes. Who are you? What do you want?'

'You won't know my name, Miss Stenning. I'm a friend of Valerie's. I believe she has phoned you?'

'Yes.' Rayne felt the hairs on the nape of her neck move slightly; there was a sense of warning which she could not explain.

'She asked you to join her here in Lugano, I understand?'

'Yes, that's so. I—' Involuntarily Rayne clamped her lips on the words she would have spoken. She would not provide this unknown caller with the fact that within a few hours she would be on her way.

'She wanted me to call you and tell you that there's no need to come out now. She's accepted an invitation to join some friends for a house party at one of the villas.'

'I see ... But—' Rayne hesitated—'why hasn't she called me herself? And what is your name?'

'My name really doesn't matter.' He sounded bored, weary; it was as if Rayne's questions were too trivial to bother to answer. 'Just don't come out here, Miss Stenning. You'll be wasting your time.'

'But I can go and stay somewhere near Valerie if you'll only give me the name and address of her friends, Mr Whoever-you-are. Only last night she was very anxious for me to go out to Switzerland. I can't understand why she should have changed her mind so quickly.'

'Never mind about where she's gone! Just don't trouble to come out here looking for her.' The man's voice had hardened, a less friendly note in it now. 'If you do, it may be the worse for you . . .'

Before Rayne could respond the click of the telephone receiver being replaced sounded in her ear. She felt both bewildered and—she faced it squarely—frightened. There was an element she did not understand in this mysterious telephone threat from a stranger. And—most puzzling feature of all about the affair—she could have sworn she heard a woman's soft voice and the sound of laughter in the background just before the caller put down the receiver.

Why did Rayne believe that the woman was Valerie? Why would she play such a childish trick?

Rayne was certain of only one thing. She was more determined than ever to travel to Lugano the following day.

CHAPTER TWO

Rayne took a seat in the aircraft next to the cabin window. The urge within her to be on her way had increased the sense of restlessness within her until it had the impetus of a driving force. Again and again she remembered the telephone call from the mysterious stranger and it filled her heart with a strange fear she was unwilling to put into words.

She was impatient to be on her way; each hour which passed until she could actually visit the Hotel Bon Accord and see if Valerie had left a forwarding address, seemed to have taken on the length of eternity itself.

Preoccupied by her anxiety for her cousin's safety she paid little attention to the tall man who took the seat beside her. It was not until he retrieved her paperback book from the aircraft floor where it had slipped unobserved by her, that she turned to look at him.

She felt almost startled by the sharply perceptive green eyes which gazed levelly back into her own. The strong features could not come into the category of handsome but there was an attractive quality in the line of his firm mouth above the deeply cleft chin. He had the appearance of leading an outdoor life if Rayne were to judge by his tanned skin and the fine lines around his eyes which usually betokened a yachtsman; his hair was dark and an unruly lock fell forward over an intelligent brow. He pushed it back with a casual gesture as if it was an annoyance he was well accustomed to.

'Are you fond of Rudyard Kipling's work?' he asked, glancing at the cover of the book as he handed it to her.

'Yes, most of it anyway,' she said, thanking him with a smile.

'My sister is one of his most ardent fans,' he responded. 'Time to fasten our seat-belts. May I help you?'

Without waiting for an answer he reached over and clipped her seat-belt fast. Rayne could smell the after-shave on his skin and, as he fastened his own belt, she observed the excellent cut of the grey suit which he wore with casual elegance. She noticed he had a briefcase on his lap as if he had papers he intended to study during the flight.

She felt the throb of the engine as it burst into life and, briefly, her pulse raced with a sudden excitement. She looked out of the cabin window and, as she did so, the plane started to move. She was on her way; within a matter of hours she would be in Lugano and—she breathed a silent prayer—surely Valerie would have left an address at the hotel where she had been staying.

The plane was airborne now. She unfastened her seat-belt and glanced down at the patchwork fields below; the river ran like a silver ribbon winding and twisting through the green and brown countryside.

'Is Zurich your destination or are you travelling on from there?' her companion asked, his words interrupting her silent reverie.

'I'm going to Lugano,' she said. 'I hope I'll be able to catch a train which will get me there later today but, if not, I shall stay in Zurich overnight and travel tomorrow morning.'

He smiled. 'Now I know it's a holiday that's taking you to Switzerland.'

'Why should you assume that?'

'Because Lugano is the holidaymaker's Mecca.'

'Perhaps . . . But I suppose one may have other, less obvious, reasons for a visit there.' Rayne's voice contained a note of asperity. She resented her companion's interest. She wished that he would open his briefcase and get on with his own affairs while she pretended to read her book. She wanted to sort out her thoughts, reflect once again on the peculiar events of the last two days.

'True. By the way, let me introduce myself . . . I'm Dean Kenton.'

He waited, eyeing her expectantly, clearly sure that she would respond with her own name. Rayne sighed. She felt she had no alternative without deliberately snubbing him.

'How do you do. I'm Rayne Stenning,' she answered.

Purposefully she opened her book and started to read, hoping that he would take the hint.

'Rayne Stenning . . .' he repeated thoughtfully. 'Now that name has a familiar ring about it. Have I seen it on book jackets?'

'You must be very observant. Yes, I have done a few illustrations for publishers.'

Rayne felt surprised and, she admitted it to herself, slightly flattered. Few people ever really noticed the tiny inscription in the corner of her work. It was pleasant to meet a member of the public who seemed to be acquainted with it. Momentarily she forgot the reason for her presence here and the sense of danger diminished as the tension within her eased. Modesty had always overridden any conceit she might have experienced in her work; always super critical of her own abilities she was more aware of her failures than her successes.

'So . . . it's to be a working holiday, is it?'

How persistent he was with his suppositions and questions! The earlier irritation rose again, quelling the unaccustomed gratification brought about by his recognition of her artistic talent.

'How very interested you do seem to be in my plans, Mr Kenton. I can't see why it should matter to you whether it's a working holiday or not.'

'Please call me Dean,' he said, his voice was smooth, his smile casual. 'Forgive me if I seem to be prying into your affairs. It's simply that I may be travelling down to Lugano myself within the next few days. It depends how

14

quickly I can complete my business in Zurich.'

'So *you* are not planning a complete escape from routine.' Rayne decided to counter his curiosity with an equal display of interest in his reasons for leaving London. 'I thought perhaps the briefcase—' her glance flicked over it as it rested on his lap—'looked a little too businesslike for a holidaymaker.'

'Let me say that it's my intention to combine business *and* pleasure.' He smiled charmingly, his manner urbane, almost deferential. 'I wondered if you would tell me where you plan to stay then maybe—' he hesitated—'I could give you a ring and take you out to a meal.'

'That's kind of you, Mr Kenton, but—'

'Dean, *please*,' he cut in. 'I do hope we're going to be friends and surnames are so formal, aren't they?' Again that swift smile and the self-deprecating expression.

'Very well. *Dean.*' Rayne was aware of the irritation in her tone. She had no time to spare for strangers at the present moment. The thought paramount in her mind was Valerie and the strange circumstances which had brought about this hurried trip to Switzerland. 'As I was saying, I'm not certain where I shall be staying in Lugano.'

'You mean you haven't made a booking?'

'No.'

'Then let's hope you will be lucky enough to obtain a cancellation. I'm afraid you've underestimated the popularity of Lugano.

15

Holidays need a little more organization than you've evidently given to this one.'

'It's not altogether a holiday. I'm joining my cousin out there. She phoned me and said she wanted to see me urgently.' *No need to tell this stranger of the second telephone call purporting to come from Valerie but about which Rayne had such doubts.*

'Then no doubt she will arrange accommodation for you,' he said smoothly, the concern he had expressed now receding from his features.

'Yes, I—I hope so.' Rayne's hesitation showed and Dean Kenton cast her a swift glance although he made no comment. She went on: 'She is staying at the Hotel Bon Accord. Do you know it?' *Never mind that it might not be strictly true that Valerie was there!*

'Yes, a charming hotel overlooking the lake. Quite small but the standards are excellent. You should be well catered for during your stay.'

'Good,' Rayne commented automatically. For a moment she was almost tempted to confide in this stranger.

There was an air of competence about him which might bolster her own swiftly decreasing confidence in the wisdom of travelling to another country on what might prove to be a wild goose chase. She resisted the temptation. She was perfectly capable of making her own decisions without listening to the advice of those who knew nothing of the situation, wasn't she? She was not normally lacking in resolution.

Exasperated with herself she returned her attention to her book and stared at the printed page, pretending to read; the words were merely black patterns on the white surface of the paper. She did not wish to continue these enforced confidences and hoped that her fellow-traveller would take the hint and leave her in silence to concentrate on her thoughts.

'This your first visit to the *Ticino* then?' He was not to be so easily put off.

Rayne stifled a weary sigh as she answered: 'I've been to Switzerland but never travelled down to the Italian border.'

'Then you're in for a completely delightful experience. You'll lose your heart to it.'

Rayne laughed. 'I keep a much tighter rein on my heart than that,' she quipped, turning back to her book.

'I must bear that in mind as a warning,' he said lightly.

Rayne shot him a swift glance but Dean's face was bland, impassive. She decided he had spoken facetiously in order to provoke a smile from her. She was not altogether amused. She resented the manner in which he had assumed their relationship would continue. She was not in the habit of picking up travelling companions and keeping them as lifelong buddies and she did not understand why Dean

Kenton should be so ready to presume on what after all were only conventional good manners.

'Yes, I should if I were you.' She tried to keep her own tone as light, flippant, as his had been.

She wished this flight were over but a peep at her wrist-watch and she saw that she still had another hour at least to endure of this frivolous chatter. Impatience flooded her in a wave. The urge to be with Valerie filled Rayne to the exclusion of all else.

The meal she was served with on the flight went scarcely tasted by her. The solicitude shown by Dean Kenton was an added source of irritation. He continued to make polite conversation to which she scarcely responded. He appeared not to notice, however, chatting companionably without seeming to expect an answer from her. After a time she stopped listening to him even, concentrating on her plans when they reached Zurich. She hoped there would be no delay at the airport and she could make good her prompt escape from this man who seemed to have appointed himself her guardian and protector.

To Rayne's relief she saw that it was time to fasten their seat-belts. At last the seemingly unending flight must be nearing its destination.

Dean once more assisted her to clip the belt, asking her if she were nervous about landing.

'Of course not!' Rayne smiled. She had the impression that if she had admitted to even the minutest degree of nerves he would have held her hand until they were on terra firma! Amusement helped to override the irritation. Not for the world would she have confessed to that momentary qualm which had snaked through her as the aircraft started its descent. She was certainly being made to feel like some fragile maiden from the nineteenth century by this man. She must pull herself together or the illusion he was encouraging might turn into a reality and her usual resourcefulness prove to be a negative passivity and acceptance.

Customs clearance was swift and efficient. The bus journey to Zurich equally speedy. Dean Kenton made sure he sat beside her but, with their ultimate destination now almost in sight, Rayne felt more kindly disposed towards him, responding to his comments on the passing scenery as they drove swiftly towards the *Bahnhof*, even interposing one or two questions of her own.

Outside the large railway station as they waited for the driver of the bus to unload their luggage, Rayne prepared herself to fend off any future suggestions of a meeting which Dean might proffer. She wanted to leave herself unfettered by any future arrangements. To her surprise and, secretly, her inner chagrin he made no reference to any further meetings. Apparently her lack of encouragement had met with more success than she had believed, she told herself, feeling a flicker of amusement. In

19

fact—and this struck her with tangible force—
Dean Kenton seemed eager now to be about
his own business; there was a patent lack of
interest in Rayne's immediate plans now that
they had set foot in Zurich.

He was given his suitcase first and, after
signalling for a taxi, it was almost cursorily that
he took her hand in his.

'It's been really nice travelling out here with
you, Rayne. Thanks for the chat. I hope you
have a good holiday with Valerie in Lugano. I'll
be thinking of you.'

It was only as he stepped inside the waiting
taxi that Rayne wondered how he could have
known her cousin's name was Valerie.

She had not mentioned it.

CHAPTER THREE

Again and again Rayne pondered the past
conversation she had had with Dean Kenton as
the train sped on its way down to the *Ticino*.
She was sure she had not mentioned her
cousin's name to him so how had he—
supposedly a stranger—come to say 'I hope you
have a good holiday with Valerie'?

Icy fingers touched her with a thrill akin to
fear. She recalled the persistence her fellow-
traveller had displayed in his questions. Had he
perhaps had some ulterior motive she had not
suspected? And why had he appeared to lose

interest in her as soon as they had arrived in Zurich?

The questions were unceasing, refusing even to be silenced by the picturesque views which each kilometre of the railway track offered to the train's passengers. Lakes and waterfalls, tumbling down from craggy mountains, sparkling in the sunlight as if bespattered with a billion sequins; tiny wooden houses like cuckoo clocks, *duvets* and bedding hanging from the windows to freshen in the champagne-like purity of the air; snow-capped mountains like pictures on a chocolate box.

She admired it with only half of her attention. The nearer the train took her to Lugano the greater became the tension within her as she recalled the telephone call which had warned her not to seek her cousin in Switzerland. The threat in the mysterious caller's message did not frighten Rayne. What did perturb her was that something unpleasant might have happened to Valerie. Perhaps she had become involved with some unsavoury characters. Recalling one or two incidents in her cousin's life Rayne felt that she would not be surprised if her cousin's indiscretion had led her into a situation which had become too difficult for her to handle alone.

The hours of the journey seemed to pass with excessive slowness despite the diversions offered by the changing scenery and the unruliness of her thoughts. She would soon be reunited with Valerie, she tried to reassure herself. When she heard the explanation for Valerie's urgent summons and the apparent change of heart, Rayne was sure she would laugh at her present fears. Fears she did not put into words even to herself . . .

Subtly the scenery had changed now; the harsh, snowy mountain ranges had given way to softer outlines. They sloped more gently upwards to the summit with verdant greenness, dotted here and there with patches of various white, blue and red wild flowers. Rayne did not recognise them all, but found that her anxious thoughts were distracted from her problems as she tried to name a few of them. The quality of light itself seemed to have changed, too. There was a mellow warmth in the sunlight and it cast a luminous golden halo on all that it touched.

Bellinzona now. The nearer they drew to Lugano the greater became Rayne's secret apprehension. The puzzle with which Dean Kenton had provided her slipped to the back of her mind now that she was faced with the prospect of being reunited with Valerie. There was surely a rational explanation for his familiarity with her cousin's name and it could only be that she—Rayne—had inadvertently mentioned it and had forgotten it.

Deliberately she told herself that she was now looking for mystery where there was no mystery to be found. Perhaps that was what she had done from the very beginning. Perhaps she

22

should have listened to the stranger who had purported to be a friend of Val's and never set out on this journey at all! Suppose it should all turn out to be a wild goose chase and her cousin had merely obeyed an impulsive whim in phoning her before she changed her mind and went off with other friends of hers!

For the first time Rayne began to regret her own impulse to come here. But after all, if she did not meet Valerie what did it really matter? Lugano would still offer a pleasant resort in which to spend a few days' vacation . . .

She closed her eyes, deliberately willing herself to relax and feeling the tension ease itself from her body. She needed a break from routine and this place must be as good as any in which to recuperate her energies after the busy rush of her daily life.

She must have dozed a little to wake with a start as she heard the sound of her fellow-passengers gathering together their luggage as the train stopped at Lugano.

They had arrived! She jumped hastily to her feet, collecting her suitcase from the rack and then alighting on the station platform. Her first impression was that she had never before in her life seen such a spanking clean railway station! The brightly coloured flowers seemed to form a welcoming party for the tourists arriving at the destination. But this was not the time to stand staring about her at the numerous distractions, she told herself firmly. The

23

immediate task was to make her way to the station exit where she would hire a taxi to take her to the Hotel Bon Accord.

Outside the station she paused, gazing about her for a moment with an expression of wonder in her eyes. Perched high on the hill the station afforded her an outlook over the panoply of sloping, tiled roofs and pink-washed walls; trees, verdant and burgeoning, spoke of the semi-tropical climate in which they flourished and the mauve bougainvillaea cascaded over a nearby wall; tiny lizards basked in the sun, darting into the crevices of walls and steps when their privacy was disturbed by the presence of those who drew too close for comfort.

Rayne felt as if a magic spell hung over the entire atmosphere of this town and, even in these first moments of her introduction to it, she felt herself falling under its hypnotic charm.

Summoning a taxi, she forced herself to make the practical efforts necessary to complete the last stage of this journey, but as she was driven swiftly towards the lakeside, she still gazed eagerly from the windows at the sights which met her no matter where she turned her attention.

The lake itself was blue as the cerulean-blue sky above, dotted with a host of small, coloured craft skimming and darting across its tranquil surface. The surrounding mountains rose in graceful splendour from the water itself, reminding her of elegant old ladies paddling their feet in the cool shallows. She could see the line of the funicular wending its snaking way upwards to the summit of San Salvatore; she resolved she would ascend the mountain if she had sufficient time during her sojourn here. The views which the trip would offer to the passenger must surely make the ascent worthwhile.

Encompassed by all that was so new and unexpected the journey to the Hotel Bon Accord passed all too quickly for Rayne. Her first glimpse of the hotel, however, reassured her. It was not so large or impressive as many they had passed on the way here, but there was a welcoming appearance in the pristine white of the building itself with the window-boxes all displaying a mixed conglomeration of colours to attract the beholder. A few rooms had balconies from which greenery and more of the ubiquitous bougainvillaea trailed, and a wide terrace, containing lounge chairs and tables, fronted the entrance itself up four stone steps.

Pleased at this first impression of the Hotel Bon Accord, Rayne looked at the outside of the building as the taxi-driver retrieved her suitcase from the luggage compartment. The hotel door-keeper made his way from the revolving doors of the hotel, smiling welcomingly as he politely greeted her.

'*Buon giorno, Signorina,*' he said, taking her

case and leading the way into the hotel.

She crossed towards the reception desk, eager now to find out if Valerie had left a forwarding address or not. It was only now that Rayne realized how anxious she secretly felt; she had refused to admit even to herself the strange disquiet which filled her.

She thrust the emotions aside, concentrating on the immediate task ahead which was, of course, to book herself into this charming hotel for a few days.

She refused to allow herself to speculate on Dean Kenton's pessimistic fears that she might have more difficulty than she had anticipated in obtaining accommodation in this busy holiday centre.

The uniformed receptionist was speaking on the telephone but she acknowledged Rayne's presence with a smile and a slight nod as if to assure her of her prompt attention. Rayne took advantage of the enforced wait to sum up the entrance hall of this pleasant hotel. Large, but not so large as to be overpowering, it was furnished with comfortable armchairs, low tables and masses of flowers set in niches against the pine panelwork of the walls. A man and his wife sat in a windowed recess; the man was reading *Le Monde* and the woman held a copy of *Paris Match* in her hand although she was occupied in looking out of the window at this moment with, Rayne considered, a rather wistful expression on her features, as if she secretly wanted to be out of doors on this glorious day.

At this hour in the afternoon it was exceedingly quiet here in the hotel; the majority of holidaymakers would be taking advantage of the numerous distractions which Lugano offered.

Her thoughts were interrupted by the softly spoken greeting of the receptionist. Rayne acknowledged it and in halting Italian she started to ask the question which had dogged her ever since she had left London.

'Per favore, mi sapreste dire se—'

The telephone bell rang and the receptionist shrugged slightly with a murmur of apology before she lifted the receiver. The call was brief and when she returned to the desk she said in English: 'Please excuse me, *Signorina*. I am on duty alone this afternoon. My colleague has gone to visit a sick *zia* . . . aunt.'

Rayne smiled to herself, both at the familiarity of the excuse and the fact that she herself must be so transparently British! But at least it helped to make matters easier.

'Can you tell me if Miss Palmer is still booked in here?'

'Miss Palmer . . .' A puzzled frown drew the girl's dark brows together as she repeated the name. *'Palmer?* I am sorry I do not recognize this name. When did she arrive?'

A coldness gripped Rayne in spite of the warmth of the day.

'I don't know exactly but she telephoned me

27

from this hotel two days ago.'

The receptionist turned back the pages of the visitors' book, flicking swiftly through them before crossing over to a filing cabinet on the far side of the desk. She fingered through the cards once then, the frown deepening, she started to go through them again, more slowly this time.

Rayne's heart sank as the receptionist glanced at her, closed the file and then moved towards her, a regretful expression in her eyes.

'I am sorry, *Signorina*, but there is nobody of that name staying here at present.'

'She is ... she must be—or, at least, she *was* staying here.' Anxiety sharpened Rayne's tones; her thoughts were a confused jumble, making it difficult to assemble her sentences together coherently. 'She phoned me from the Hotel Bon Accord. She asked me to join her here. Is there another hotel of the same name in Lugano?'

'No, *Signorina*, but you must be mistaken in the name of your friend's hotel because there is no *Signorina* Palmer registered here.'

'She's my cousin.' The remark was irrelevant but Rayne was too worried to care. 'I must find her.'

The receptionist's earlier concern had given way to a vague air of disinterest and boredom. Rayne had the impression that the pretty girl was wondering if she—Rayne—was a crank to be treated with patient tolerance. She must meet many eccentrics in her place behind the hotel desk. Rayne wondered how she could convince her of her own genuine puzzled sense of bewilderment.

'Forgive me! I'm sorry to be so insistent but you must have made a mistake in her name or—or something.'

'*Signorina*, I assure you there is no mistake made.' The girl's voice was cool now, the earlier friendliness dispersed under Rayne's persistence. 'There is no name which even resembles Palmer in our list of guests nor has there been for several months.'

Could Valerie have booked in under an assumed name? The idea struck Rayne forcibly.

'Perhaps she—' Rayne paused, wondering how to phrase the question. She decided to start it again. 'Do you have a guest who resembles *me* in any way?—no matter what her name!'

The receptionist was by now clearly convinced that Rayne was out of her wits and merely shook her head, glancing at the telephone as if willing it to ring and release her from this unwelcome inquisition. Rayne intercepted the expression and felt her hackles begin to rise in angry self-defence.

'I do assure you I'm perfectly sane,' she said coldly. 'I also assure you that my cousin telephoned me the night before last and begged me to join her at the Hotel Bon Accord in Lugano as soon as possible. I am here. Now where is she? I'm determined to find her.'

'Do you think she plays a joke on you, yes?' enquired the receptionist, her manner now slightly more placatory as if Rayne's obvious annoyance had convinced her of her sincerity.

'No.' But although the monosyllable shot out with force Rayne could not be certain. Valerie had always been unpredictable.

'There is no single lady staying here at present ... Just single gentlemen and a few married couples. Perhaps a visit to the *questura* ... the police-station would be indicated, Signorina?'

'Yes, perhaps. But, meanwhile—' Rayne held her breath for a moment—'do you have a single room vacant that I could have? I had believed my cousin would have made a reservation for me so I didn't bother.'

The receptionist smiled. 'You are very lucky, *Signorina*. The last telephone call I took was a cancellation. It is the only vacancy we now have. Would you like to register and take it?'

CHAPTER FOUR

Once in the room, her suitcase unpacked, Rayne stepped out on to the balcony which overlooked the lake. The water was a hive of activity and along the wide encircling promenade tourists and Luganesi alike strolled, enjoying the breeze which gently stirred through the leafy branches of the magnolia and chestnut trees. The cool shade they offered was inviting on this warm day and, even from this distance, Rayne could see the enormous creamy-white magnolia blossoms like Chinese lanterns in the greenery. She could hear the strains of a Neapolitan love song carrying across the water from one of the small passenger boats and, a trap for romantic tourists or not, she felt her heart stir to it.

It was a flower-filled town of music and laughter; it was a town for lovers and sweethearts to share an interlude from the cares of the real world.

But for Rayne it seemed that the very unreality of the place served only to stress the nightmare quality of this time.

She could scarcely believe that the Hotel Bon Accord were correct when they told her that Valerie had not been registered as a guest with them. Why should her cousin have lied to her when she had telephoned? Why had she asked her—Rayne—to meet her here? No! There had to be a logical explanation and the most likely one was that the receptionist had made a mistake.

Rayne would check again with somebody else . . . the manager perhaps. She was determined to get to the bottom of this strange business and standing here pondering over the past events was hardly the best way to do it, she chided herself.

She felt hot and sticky after her journey so decided to shower and change before once more tackling the receptionist at the desk with more questions. Slipping into a cream silk dress Rayne made a mental resolution not to allow herself to be daunted by the news that Valerie had not been here.

Perhaps—the sudden idea raced to mind and Rayne brightened at once—Valerie would contact her here herself! Yes, of course that must be what she intended to do!

Rayne felt much better now that she had thought of this. She even found herself humming a few notes of *Core 'ngrato* beneath her breath as she brushed her hair with swift strokes. Italian boatmen were not the only ones with music in their hearts! she smiled. This town was enough to make anybody sing!—even somebody as worried as she was.

The realization that she was worried stilled the impulse to make music. Suddenly Rayne knew that not only was she mystified, she felt frightened. She could not have explained why. She was aware only that her blood had turned to ice; it seemed that she was caught in a web of events which—

The telephone bell rang in her room, startling her from the labyrinth of her own thoughts. Her heart lifted in sudden hope; her face was alight with pleasure and welcome relief as she hurried across to the bedside to take the call.

'*Pronto*,' she said.

'*Signorina*,' there is a telephone call for you. One moment, please,' came the receptionist's reply.

Rayne recognized that it was the same girl she had spoken to earlier. But now all Rayne's attention was on this call as her heart beat faster in anticipation. Thank goodness! She was sure that this muddle was now about to be cleared up. Hadn't she just told herself that Valerie would get in touch with her here? Valerie was the only person who was likely to know she was staying here and—

But with the spoken greeting of her caller Rayne felt her hopes dashed to the ground. Of course! Dean Kenton . . . She had forgotten him in the stress of the recent revelations which had come to light since she had left him in Zurich.

'Hello, Rayne. I was wondering if you'd managed to get booked in all right. I know now that you have. Is everything to your satisfaction?' His voice was cool, assured.

'Oh, hello!' She tried to conceal the momentary disappointment she had felt in the identity of her caller. 'Yes, thank you,' she went on. 'I was lucky that there was a cancellation and I arrived in time to obtain it.'

'Your guardian angel must have been watching over you,' he said easily. 'How's your cousin? Pleased to see you?'

'N-no.' Rayne hesitated. Should she tell him

33

all that had transpired or should she maintain her discretion . . .? It was a difficult decision. 'She—she's not here,' she answered, after a pause.

'Oh? You mean she's out at the moment and you haven't seen her yet?' The question came sharply.

'I mean she's just not here.'

'You've missed her? She's left? Did she leave a forwarding address?'

Rayne sighed. She might as well tell this inquisitive stranger and get it over! His persistence was remarkable!

'According to the hotel's records she's never stopped here at all.'

'Then you must have been mistaken in the name of the hotel,' he said flatly.

'That's what they said too,' she retorted expressionlessly.

'But you don't believe that you are . . .?'

'I know she told me the Hotel Bon Accord. Unless there's another hotel of the same name in Lugano . . . and the receptionist here said there isn't one . . . then she should be here . . . or, at least, she should have been registered here.'

'You're worried, aren't you?'

'Wouldn't you be in the circumstances?'

'I already am . . . . about *you*, Rayne.'

'What do you mean? Why should you be worried about me?'

'You seem to have a knack for impulsive

34

behaviour which can land you in trouble.'

'What are you talking about?'

'I find it somewhat astonishing that you came out to Switzerland on the first flight available just because your cousin rings you and tells you that she needs to see you.' He waited; the silence lengthened, became almost tangible.

'Then perhaps you underestimate my affection for my cousin ... which, of course, would scarcely be surprising since you hardly know me.' She spoke in honeyed tones which did not reflect the sharp thrust of anger which pierced through her.

'A pity it seems not to be returned by her.'

'What do you mean?'

'She seems not to have any qualms about bringing you here on a wild goose chase ... I do wonder *why* we call it a "wild goose chase"?' he added speculatively, as an afterthought.

'*We* don't call it any such thing, Dean,' retaliated Rayne sharply. 'I know my cousin must have been staying here ... I also know she must have needed me. I intend staying here and finding out why ... And another thing—' she went on quickly, suddenly remembering the odd fact which had perplexed her in Zurich—'how did you know my cousin's name was Valerie? I never mentioned it.'

'Did I know it?' he countered, his manner easy and unruffled. 'Are you sure you didn't tell me? I really don't remember.'

'Well, I do remember. You did and *I* didn't,' she flared at him.

He laughed. 'The grammatical construction of that sentence seems to lack a certain clarity, Rayne. I can only suggest my psychic faculties must have been working in top gear.'

'I don't believe you.'

'You have a charming pithiness in your comments.' There was a hint of amusement in his tones. 'Anyway—' his voice sharpened, becoming serious once more—'what are your immediate plans?'

Rayne, sitting on the bed, clasping the telephone receiver to her ear, looked out of the window and over the expanse of blue water. She could see Monte Generoso opposite, a few fluffy white clouds around the summit as if the mountain wore a necklace of pearls. How peaceful and serene it looked from this distance.

She dragged her errant thoughts back from their subconscious attempt to escape the necessity of answering Dean Kenton's question. She wished that she knew herself what her immediate plans were! The one course of action she knew she would not take, however, was to return to England without making some effort to trace Valerie. To do so would be tantamount to confessing failure—and that was not Rayne's way.

'My immediate plans are to go down to the dining-room and order something to eat,' she

36

answered lightly. 'I'm hungry! So, if you'll excuse me, Dean, I will wish you a pleasant stay in Switzerland and—'

'No, wait!' he said urgently. 'Rayne, listen! Go home. You shouldn't have come out here in the first place and—'

'Are you warning me off?' Her tone sharpened, she felt an icy touch of fear once more. Was this the second attempt to frighten her and prevent her seeking Valerie? 'Who are you really . . .? What's all this about . . .?'

'Don't be ridiculous! How melodramatic! Why should you think I know anything about it? I simply don't like the idea of you being alone in Lugano and anxious about your cousin's whereabouts—as you clearly are. She's more likely to try to contact you at home in England than anywhere, isn't she?'

'No. I think she will try to reach me here—' she added slowly—'if she can.'

'What do you mean by "if she can"?'

'I'm beginning to think that—' Rayne paused, running her tongue across lips gone suddenly dry— 'that Valerie has been abducted by—by somebody. I'm also convinced, Mr Dean Kenton, that you know more about it all than you are telling me in spite of your denials.'

'You've been watching too much television,' he mocked gently.

Rayne felt uncomfortable. Was she being foolish? Self-doubt consumed her for a moment before that sliver of suspicion once

37

more strengthened.

'I suppose I should have expected you to say something like that,' she retorted.

'Don't you think that you are maybe being a little paranoic, Rayne?' he enquired.

Rayne sensed an underlying seriousness in his tones now. Or was it annoyance? Perhaps he was angry with her for her suggestion that he was not being completely straightforward with her.

'I don't know what to think any more,' she admitted, after a brief silence. 'I only know that I must try to find Valerie. I'm sure she needs me badly. She's in trouble of some kind or another and—and I'm the only person she can turn to for help.'

Almost without realizing it Rayne repeated Valerie's pathetic words during her short telephone call to her.

'I think you're making a mistake, Rayne, but I can't stop you.'

'Too damned right!' she answered sharply. 'I'm beginning to wonder what right you think you have to interfere in my private life.'

'I only wanted to be friends but you seem to have cast me in the role of an enemy,' Dean Kenton returned shortly. 'I think your imagination has been working overtime. I can only wish you success in finding your cousin, Rayne. Enjoy your stay in Lugano. *Ciao, bella ragazza!*'

Before she could respond the soft click of

the receiver being replaced sounded in Rayne's ear. Slowly she replaced her own receiver, her eyes shadowed and her expression troubled. Dean had made no reference to any future calls or meetings and, momentarily, a stab of regret fired her.

Nevertheless, she had the strongest impression that she had not heard the last of Mr Dean Kenton. She wondered when their paths would next cross—and what would be the circumstances which would surround their meeting . . .

CHAPTER FIVE

Awaking the following morning in the hotel room which was now taking on all the familiarity of 'home' to Rayne, she reviewed the situation in which she found herself.

Reflecting on the advice given to her by Dean Kenton the previous evening she was half inclined to believe there was more than a grain of common sense in his words. Not that she would have admitted it to him for the world!

She was fast coming to the conclusion that she had been the victim of a hoax set for her by Valerie. Why her cousin should have played such a prank was far beyond Rayne's imagination, but what other reason could there be to account for the events which had taken place? It was difficult to conceive that, in this sunlit, happy holiday town, forces might be at work with less creditable motives.

The more Rayne considered the affair the more she was forced to the opinion that she had indeed over-reacted to Valerie's telephone call and the subsequent call from the stranger. Dean Kenton was right! She was being melodramatic and, momentarily, she regretted her scarcely veiled accusations of the previous evening. He had, after all, merely been showing a kind interest and the snub she had proffered was poor reward for his solicitude.

She sighed, brushing aside her vague regrets. She had spoken hastily and one would not expect him to be eager to receive another dose of the same medicine.

Rayne stepped out of bed, crossing the room to look out of the window at the pleasant early morning scene. The sun was just beginning to rise above the mountains, throwing a long sequinned ribbon of light across the smooth surface of the lake. A lone speedboat was crossing from the direction of Gandria, churning up a long trail of white spume in its wake. One dog sat beside a seat on the promenade opposite and, fleetingly, Rayne wondered if the animal belonged to the enthusiastic pilot of the speedboat; even as she watched, though, she saw two strolling figures come into view and the dog wag its tail and fall into step beside them.

It must be very early. She picked up her

wrist-watch from the dressing-table where she had left it before getting into bed the night before. Five a.m.! She grimaced slightly to herself. She had two hours to pass before she could go down to breakfast. Well, she would try to use the time sensibly and come to a decision about her next course of action.

She was beginning to agree with Dean Kenton that she would be wiser to return to London on the next flight on which she could reserve a seat.

The thought of the tedious rail journey from Lugano to Zurich and then the flight back home scarcely filled her with any great enthusiasm. She still felt travel-weary after her journey here, and the anti-climax of her arrival had done little to restore her flagging spirits. Another glance out of the window and she found the temptation to stay in Lugano for a few days almost outweighing the more sensible course of action. It would be very agreeable to spend a few days here without the commitments and pressures of her busy life. But—and she faced it squarely—she would hardly be able to relax to any great degree while worrying about Valerie. *And worry about Valerie she would until her cousin put in an appearance once again . . .*

Back to square one! she told herself in a resigned manner. Where on earth could Valerie be? . . . and what could have possessed her to act in such an irresponsible way?

41

Rayne took a leisurely shower before dressing in a pair of jeans and a blue tee-shirt. After breakfast she would take a stroll along the lakeside while she considered whether to return home or spend a few days here in this agreeable environment and hope that Valerie would try to contact her at the Hotel Bon Accord.

An hour later she was strolling along the lakeside, the fresh breeze from the water lightly ruffling her hair and the dappled sunlight warm on her face. The lake was busier now with a host of small craft plying from one landing stage to another at the mountain villages which ran around the vast circumference of the water. Campione: Morcote: Gandria. She heard a boatman calling out to attract the attention of passing tourists. The very names held music . . .

She was almost tempted to board one of the boats herself but the necessity to sort out her future plans seemed to preclude taking advantage of the leisure activities designed for holidaymakers. She smiled to herself, wondering why she drew this distinction between sauntering along this delightful promenade and sitting in the bows of a boat as it sped across the smooth surface of the lake.

She sat for a while on one of the benches beneath the magnolias; the air was heavily scented with linden and, revelling in the beauty which invaded all her senses, she felt her tension drift from her.

Rayne lost account of how long she sat on that seat but, half regretfully, she decided to find a café where she would order a *cappuccino* and continue to think out her next course of action.

She got up and strolled off, not hurrying but enjoying all the sights and sounds which offered themselves for her delectation. She turned off from the lakeside into the colonnaded centre of the town; now a hot, spicy smell of perfumes, Turkish tobacco, sausage, cheese and wines mingled in an unforgettable aroma.

She wandered from shop display to display. Coloured scarves like gaudy butterflies: leather handbags and exquisite shoes: delicate Cashmere sweaters in tempting designs and colours fragile as a rainbow. At last she found her wandering feet had brought her along the Via Nassa and outside *Vanini*'s. She went in, admiring the assortment of shiny chocolates and creamy *törtchen*. She was not hungry but the *cappuccino* was welcome and delicious.

She sat for a while in the charming surroundings but, with a glance at her wrist-watch, she saw that she had been dawdling here far longer than she had intended so, reaching for her handbag which she had placed on the vacant seat beside her, she decided to make tracks back to the hotel.

'Valerie! Where have you been hiding yourself? I tried to ring you at Marco's several times but he said he hadn't seen you either!'

The smiling-faced, dark-haired girl who stood in front of Rayne's table was clearly a friend of Valerie's and English as there was no trace of accent in her speech. Involuntarily Rayne went to explain that the other girl had made a mistake but an inner instinct suddenly prevented her. The words faded on her lips. She felt herself tense. Could she manage to get away with such a deception? It would depend how friendly this girl really was with her cousin . . . Surely she could at least *try* . . .

'Hello!' she said, her tone friendly. 'I—I've been away for a few days. I only got back last night.'

'What a stroke of luck! Are you still staying in Marco's villa?'

'No. I—I booked in at the Hotel Bon Accord!' She hoped this stranger would not try to seek Valerie Palmer there and, momentarily, regretted that she had not said she was staying with the unknown Marco. Who *were* all these people? How Rayne would like to know this girl's name!

'You *did*? Oh, what a *scream!* I shan't tell Francesco that . . . I'll let him continue to think Marco and you have more than a passing fancy for each other . . . Only the other evening he said to me "Barbara, I'll kill Marco if he harms Valerie in any way". He really does care for you, Val.'

'That's nice!'

So this girl's name was Barbara! It was an

44

answer to her unspoken wish. Rayne's mind was ticking over swiftly. This was a strange situation indeed and she wondered why she simply didn't tell Barbara the truth about her true identity.

'Did you go back to London to see that cousin of yours?'

Rayne's heart pounded. 'N-no,' she answered hesitantly. 'I didn't go there after all.'

'Just as well. Francesco wouldn't thank you for bringing in a stranger.'

'That's what I thought.' *Had it been the unknown Francesco who had phoned the flat, warning her not to come to Lugano?* 'Anyway, what do you mean about my return being "a stroke of luck"?'

'Francesco wants to see you tomorrow night, Val. He has lined up a large social occasion in the Villa Mirabella on the Gandria road. He has hired the villa especially for the occasion. Fancy dress! *You* are to attend as a Victorian flowerseller—you know, a sort of Eliza Dolittle figure.'

'Why is *he* choosing what I should attend as?' asked Rayne.

Barbara's brows drew into a frown. 'If he doesn't know what you are dressed as he might not recognize you, silly! He's not likely to take chances. He's even chosen the rendezvous with extra care.'

'The Villa Mirabella, you say?' enquired Rayne, each question she asked was a testing point.

45

'Yes, you probably know it . . .' answered Barbara. 'The villa stands back from the road and it's a discreet distance from town. I'll tell Francesco you'll be there at eight o'clock, shall I?'

Rayne nodded. 'Yes,' she answered slowly. 'Tell him I'll be there.'

With a wave of her hand Barbara departed, leaving Rayne still sitting at the table, a worried expression in her grey eyes.

She could not understand her own reluctance to tell this unknown girl Barbara, that she was not Valerie. An instinct warned her that if she admitted the truth Barbara would have clammed up at once.

At least Rayne had now established a connection between her cousin and two mysterious gentlemen named Marco and Francesco. It almost sounded to her as if Marco had a hold over Valerie which was resented by Francesco. And where did Barbara stand in all this? She had greeted Rayne, supposing her to be Valerie, with pleasant friendliness, but presumably Valerie had not felt they were very close or she would not have telephoned Rayne to ask her to come to Lugano because she had nobody to whom she could turn for help.

Rayne ordered another *cappuccino* while she reflected on the turn which events had taken in the few minutes since she had been in here. She did not want to leave yet awhile; she did not wish to run the chance of meeting Barbara outside.

She wondered if she could possibly expect to get away with masquerading as Valerie at this fancy dress party tomorrow! The deception would undoubtedly run a high risk of being unsuccessful but—

Rayne bit her lower lip anxiously. *If* she were dressed in an Eliza Dolittle bonnet this would surely conceal much of her features? And if she pretended to have a headache she need not stay too long—just long enough to recce the other guests who must be acquainted with her cousin. Perhaps, amongst them somewhere, there would be one person she could trust . . . one person who would know where Valerie was at the present moment . . .!

One thing was sure. Rayne was getting progressively more anxious about her cousin as the time passed. She knew, somewhere deep inside her, that all was not well with the other girl.

CHAPTER SIX

The Hotel Bon Accord came into sight and Rayne heaved a hearty sigh.

Strolling back here through the labyrinth of quaint streets she had found herself anxiously cogitating the practicability of the idea. Side by side with Valerie it was easier to note the differences in their appearance but, she told herself reassuringly, the unknown Barbara had

47

clearly confused her with her cousin. If the similarity in their looks was sufficient to deceive one person then surely a fancy dress party would be a walk-over?

Rayne felt her determination strengthening. After all, this would be a lead towards finding Valerie. No longer did she believe that Valerie's inexplicable vanishing act had been her cousin's idea of a practical joke. Evidently even her cousin's friends had missed her presence in their midst and had no explanation to offer for her withdrawal from society.

She increased her pace, eager now to enquire whether there had been a message left for her by her cousin while she had been absent during this morning's excursion. There was no reason to suppose there would have been but Rayne was now clutching at straws, anxious and perplexed by the chain of circumstances.

She hurried over to the reception desk to collect her room key and make her request about telephone calls.

She was disappointed. There had been no messages for her and she felt her heart sink as the male receptionist on duty regarded her almost sympathetically, an expression of understanding in his liquid dark eyes. Rayne smiled to herself. Of course he believed that it must be an affair of the heart! How mistaken he was!

She turned away from the reception desk almost into the arms of the tall man who stood waiting behind her.

'I'm so sorry,' she started to apologize, startled by the impact of the collision. 'I—' The words faded on her lips as she found herself gazing up into Dean Kenton's features. Then: '*You!*' she exclaimed, aghast. 'Whatever are *you* doing *here?*'

'I told you I might get down to Lugano if all went smoothly with my business,' he replied. 'I decided to come straight here and take you out to lunch—' he added, swiftly—'that is, if you're free, of course.'

She nodded, bemused by the unexpected meeting. She had dismissed the idea of seeing him again after last night's telephone call and his sudden appearance had provided a welcome cessation to the anxious preoccupation with the morning's events.

The receptionist was studying them both, watching Rayne in particular, as if trying to assess whether this tall Englishman was, perhaps, the one from whom she had so clearly hoped to hear. Life, as seen from behind the reception desk of any reasonably sized hotel, offered a wide panoply of romantic attachments to the observer!

Unable to dredge up any valid excuse not to accept Dean's luncheon invitation—and even unsure as to why she should wish to do so— Rayne agreed reluctantly to meet him here in the reception hall in half an hour's time.

'I'm hardly suitably dressed for a luncheon

49

date,' she smiled, casting a rueful glance down at her well-worn jeans and tee-shirt. 'I'll have to change.'

'You look pretty good to me just as you are,' returned Dean, his admiration clear in his eyes as he followed her gaze down the length of her slim figure.

'Then you show little sense of discrimination,' she retaliated, as she moved towards the lift.

The brief period before they met gave her an opportunity to gather her thoughts together and make up her mind as to exactly how much or how little she should disclose to him of the morning's happenings.

She splashed her face with cold water from the basin in her bedroom in an attempt to freshen herself after her walk in the warmth of the sun's full heat. Feeling cooler now, she changed into a green linen suit and ran a comb through her hair. She observed that the sun had already tinted her skin with delicate honey-gold tones and, slicking a rosy lipstick across her lips, knew that she needed no additional make-up.

She still had a few minutes in hand and passed it standing on the small balcony outside her room, watching the water traffic on the lake which now seemed to be buzzing with activity. For a few moments Rayne actually forgot the niggling concern she felt for Valerie as she relaxed in the carnival atmosphere which reigned on the water and by the lakeside. It was as if the worries dropped from her shoulders and she became part of the living, vibrant force around her.

She sighed, reluctant to leave her vantage point and the encompassing solitude of the balcony. She supposed she must go down to meet Dean Kenton now and still she was no nearer knowing whether or not she intended to confide in him.

She scorned the lift, choosing to make her way down the wide staircase.

Dean was standing near the swing doors, his expression serious, his eyes shaded in thoughts which were clearly occupying all his attention. But even as Rayne wondered what could be provoking such intense concentration from him, he turned and, seeing her approaching him, his features lightened into the more familiar lines of laughter.

He held out his hands to her, his lips pursed into a silent whistle of approval.

'Your own sense of discrimination, I can see, is absolutely excellent,' he complimented her. 'I shall have to fight off every red-blooded Italian male from miles around.'

He took her elbow and started to move towards the door. Rayne paused, throwing him a surprised glance from wide eyes.

'Aren't we eating here?' she asked.

'Certainly not. I want all Lugano to see you in that ravishing outfit.'

51

'Spoofer!' she laughed, passing him as she went through the door he held open for her.

He led her towards a small, low sports car parked near the entrance and she turned to him with another surprised glance.

'Hired!' he laconically answered her unspoken question. 'I picked it up in Zurich. It's a little gem.'

He drove swiftly towards the outskirts of the town. It seemed to Rayne that he must be well acquainted with this region of the *Ticino* as he displayed no hesitation in finding his way through the narrow, winding streets. He made no attempt to keep up a conversation with her, merely pointing out one or two places of particular interest as they passed, but otherwise quite content to drive in silence.

The *taverna* to which he took her was perched high on the hill above the lake; they chose a table on the verandah outside, sheltered from the sun's relentless rays by a canopy of green vines overhead. Along the surrounding wall bougainvillaea encroached in a brilliant display of colour which vied with the Madonna blue of the water and cloudless sky; hibiscus, too, bloomed profusely in a range of palest shell-pink to a deep, deep rose.

Rayne smiled gently to herself as she looked about her with wondering eyes.

'Why do you smile?' asked Dean.

'I was just thinking that if this were a painting I would believe the artist had added a few touches of his imagination and a few patches of bright colour which weren't actually there in the reality,' she answered.

'I know what you mean ... It all seems a little larger than life, doesn't it?'

Rayne nodded, suddenly losing interest in the panoramic view spread out around and below her. She had other—more pressing—problems and it seemed as if they had unexpectedly combined to bring back her wandering attention to the matter of her missing cousin.

Sensing Rayne's withdrawal Dean cast her a speculative glance from behind the ornate menu which the waiter had presented to him.

'What do you fancy to eat?' he asked her.

Rayne shrugged, her appetite had diminished and the thought of food was almost sickening to her. She wished she had not consented to come with Dean and the contrariness of her own emotions angered her. What was the matter with her? she asked herself impatiently, forcing herself to concentrate on her companion and the necessity to get through the next hour or two without giving away the true depth of her anxiety about Valerie.

'You choose for me!' she said lightly. 'You seem to be the authority around here!'

He grinned and then in fluent Italian gave their order to the waiter.

The service was swift and efficient; the food

he chose appetising and delectable; the white wine he ordered cool and refreshing. Gradually Rayne felt her inner tension dispersing in the relaxing ambience of these pleasant surroundings. It was with a sense of shock she found herself suddenly confronted by Dean's blunt question.

'Any news of Valerie? Has she tried to contact you yet?'

Rayne shook her head, her indecision mounting. Could she really trust this man who seemed to know more than he had revealed to her about her cousin?

'No, not yet,' she answered, almost unwillingly.

'You still think she's going to?'

'Why shouldn't she?' Rayne spoke defensively. 'She asked me to join her here.'

'And also, if I understand you correctly, led you to believe she was staying in a hotel which has no record of a visitor bearing her name!'

Rayne shifted uncomfortably in her seat. He was right, of course!

'There's something terribly wrong, Dean,' she burst out, almost surprising herself by the wealth of relief she experienced as she shed the load of her problem. 'I believe Valerie is in trouble of some sort and I must try to help her.'

'I would have thought you would have been in a better situation to help her back home.'

'I can't see how you figure that out. I'm nearer to her here.'

'And I can't see quite how *you* figure that out. You haven't seen her here yet and, for all you know, she may have returned to England.'

'I don't think so.'

'What makes you say that?' demanded Dean Kenton sharply.

Suddenly Rayne found herself telling him all about the strange meeting of the morning in *Vanini's*. She tried to describe the unknown Barbara to him but, even as she did so, realized that the girl's features were now only a shadowy memory. Would she—Rayne—even recognize her again if they met . . .? Her emotions rose in an almost tangible miasma of fear, clutching her heart in cold and icy dread.

They had reached the coffee stage of their meal now and Dean Kenton thoughtfully spooned sugar into his cup as he asked: 'And your mad idea is to pretend to be Valerie and go to this—' he paused, his tone and manner disapproving—'fancy dress affair?'

She nodded eagerly. 'It's a link, don't you see? And at least I shall be able to meet a few of her friends and acquaintances.'

'Madness!' he snapped. 'I beg you, go home, Rayne, before you get into a mess you can't handle.'

'Then you admit there's something wrong?' she declared, almost triumphantly.

'I admit no such thing. I think your imagination is working overtime.'

'Then why do you talk about "getting into a

mess I can't handle"?' she demanded.

He sighed heavily, speaking patiently as if to a child. 'My dear Rayne, I—'

'I'm neither yours nor dear to you,' she interrupted sharply. 'Don't patronize me.'

'I'm sorry, I'm just convinced your imagination is playing you tricks and you're making a mountain out of a molehill.'

'If you've finished with the clichés, do you think we might return to the hotel now, Dean?'

She pushed her half finished coffee and untouched liqueur away from her, suddenly filled with an intuitive and urgent need to be back at the Hotel Bon Accord. She should never have left it! Suppose Valerie were trying to contact her there at this very moment?

'As you wish, Rayne.' He spoke almost coldly, signalling to the waiter for the check. 'I think you're being singularly stupid and, to use another cliché, jumping in where angels fear to tread. I'm afraid you're stepping into a situation you won't be able to handle.'

'But if it's all down to my overworked imagination,' she retorted, in honeyed tones, 'I can't really see that I'm stepping into any situation, Dean. You seem to be contradicting yourself, but don't worry, I'll be careful.'

They drove back to the Hotel Bon Accord in silence and Dean stopped the car outside; he did not enter the foyer with her. He made no reference to any further meeting and, taking her hand as they stood on the pavement beside the car, he bent forward and kissed her lightly on the cheek.

'Loyal Rayne!' he commented. 'I hope your cousin appreciates what a good friend you are. I hope you find her soon, my dear. *Ciao!*'

Before Rayne could respond he had stepped into the low-slung car and switched on the engine. With a wave of his hand he had driven off, out of sight . . . *Out of her life?* she suddenly asked herself, and was surprised by the unexpected sense of loneliness which assailed her.

CHAPTER SEVEN

Finding a theatrical costumiers in a foreign country was not one of the easiest tasks, but Rayne at last succeeded in tracing a small firm and hiring a Victorian gown, bonnet and flower basket filled with a wide variety of silk flowers.

Donning the heavy petticoats and the black crinoline gown, decorated with mauve ribbons, she felt excitement snake within her. For a second she wondered if she were being wise in attending this function at the Villa Mirabella but she thrust the timorous doubts away.

She was allowing Dean Kenton's disapproval to cloud her own judgement and she felt angry at herself for the doubts which rose within her from time to time.

There had been no further word from Dean since he had brought her back to the hotel the previous day. She had not really expected to hear from him again. His parting words had sounded strangely final to her ears. She wished that she could have made him understand her desperate need to do all that was in her power to contact Valerie herself, but she knew that a stranger would not truly comprehend the sense of responsibility she felt for her cousin's welfare. They shared an unusual relationship; closer than the usual cousinly link because of the similarity in their looks and the fact that they had both been orphaned so early in their lives.

She gazed at her reflection in the mirror, feeling as if she were staring at a stranger in the unusual garb. The anxiety which shadowed her eyes gave her a waif-like appearance and, as she picked up her basket of silken posies, she almost felt she had stepped back in time, back to another existence as fraught with problems as her present-day life seemed to be at this period.

Rayne hired a taxi to take her to the Villa Mirabella and as the driver wound his way through the intertwining streets behind the Castagnola end of the lake, she felt herself gradually becoming more and more nervous. She must be mad, she told herself, even to hope she'd get away with this impersonation to Valerie's friends!

The two-storeyed villa stood in its own grounds, remote from the iron gates of the entrance. Lights poured from the windows and open doorway, throwing a glowing golden carpet down the driveway; sounds of music drifted from the house and several cars were parked outside; from one of them Rayne observed a tall Indian gentleman climbing out. His white turban hit the car roof as he did so and he hastily put up his hand to catch it before it fell off.

Rayne smiled to herself as she paid off her taxi and started to make her way inside. Several of the party-goers attired in various manners of fancydress greeted her with a smile and wave of the hand. One girl, dressed as Little Bo-Peep, called out to her to grab herself a drink from one of the waiters passing amongst the guests with loaded trays.

Rayne did not know if they were friends of Valerie's or if they were merely being hospitable to their fellow-guests but, taking a drink, she stood at the side of the room watching the flow of the guests as they drifted in chattering profusion from one group to another.

She found herself being drawn into a circle comprised of Oliver Cromwell, Henry VIII and Anne Boleyn and, incongruously, Peter Pan. The conversation was general. Henry VIII was intent on telling jokes in a long-winded fashion and, as unobtrusively as she was able, Rayne disentangled herself from their midst and wandered amongst the ever-increasing press of

59

visitors.

The evening drew on. She felt her apprehension increasing as it seemed there was to be no event which would lead her any nearer to finding Valerie. She was beginning to wonder if Dean Kenton was right. Perhaps it would be better if she were to return back home and wait for news of Valerie there. She seemed to be wasting here doing her 'private detective' act. In fact the more she thought about it, the more foolish she was beginning to feel! What did she hope to gain by all this? And where was this mysterious Francesco who had ordered what fancy dress guise Valerie was to wear to this exceedingly expensive 'do' this evening?

Rayne's thoughts raced over and over the same tracks as she chatted to various guests. At one point she plucked up courage to ask if her companion—a rather modern day Mary, Queen of Scots—had seen any signs of Francesco about. The reply had done little to boost Rayne's confidence that this evening would produce any results leading to Valerie's whereabouts.

'Francesco? Oh, I haven't seen him about yet. But you know how unpredictable he can be! Throws a party for us all and then doesn't turn up himself! He's done it before so there's no reason to suppose he won't be doing it again this evening . . . Just have a good time and—' a

tinkle of laughter accompanied the words—
' drink all the champagne available but don't
question where your host has vanished to.'

Looking about her Rayne could not see any
glimpse of Barbara either, although it might
not be easy to recognize her amongst the
assorted identities of the guests.

The numbers in the room seemed constantly
to increase and the atmosphere was growing
hot and oppressive; tobacco smoke mingled
with cloying perfumes and Rayne felt the first
warnings of a throbbing headache. She wished
she could get a little fresh air and started to
weave amongst the guests in the direction of
the open French doors which led to the terrace
beyond.

'Valerie! Valerie . . .!'

The voice which came from behind her filled
her with a sudden, almost overwhelming desire
to escape from this room. She prayed fleetingly
for the ability to carry through this task which
she had set for herself. Not for the first time
she found herself regretting the fact that she
had not taken Dean Kenton's well-meant
advice and returned home immediately. She
was beginning to feel out of her depths now
and, even as she turned to confront the person
who spoke, she had to force a smile to her lips.

'Oh, hello!' she said. 'I—I didn't see you.'

The man who faced her, attired in a Roman
toga which well suited the darkness of his
classic features, smiled enigmatically.

'You were deep in contemplation, were you not?' His voice was deep, his accent barely noticeable. 'What were you thinking of, *cara mia*?'

'The—the room was so crowded . . . I came over a little faint . . .' It was a lie but it would serve to excuse the fact that she had passed within a hair's breadth of this man who clearly seemed to know Valerie intimately. Was this the mysterious Francesco?

The question was answered for her by another passing guest who called out:

'Great party, Francesco. Thanks for inviting me.'

Francesco merely smiled, returning his attention to Rayne, his keen look scrutinizing her so closely she felt a thrill of apprehension stir within her. *Did he guess that she was not Valerie?*

'How well your costume becomes you!'

'How well you chose for me, Francesco!' she answered lightly.

'As you know, I have long believed that flowers and you are kindred souls. It is difficult to know which is truly the more beautiful.'

'Such flattery warms my heart even if I'm well aware you don't mean one word of it,' she responded, with a laugh.

He raised a quizzical eyebrow. 'You don't usually disbelieve my compliments, Valerie.' He sounded slightly questioning.

Rayne caught her breath sharply. Evidently

62

she was not behaving in the typical way Valerie would have done. She must be extra careful if she were not to arouse this man's suspicions.

'But—' he gripped her arm tightly and Rayne winced slightly at the pressure of his strong fingers—'you are feeling a little unwell, you say? Come, *bambina*! Let us go outside on the terrace.'

Heart beating rapidly she allowed Francesco to lead her towards the French doors. It was less crowded outside and the cool night air felt pleasant on Rayne's hot cheeks. He indicated a vacant bench and they moved towards it. A few other guests had had the same idea of escaping from the overheated atmosphere of the rooms inside and Rayne was grateful for their proximity. If only she knew the relationship which existed between her cousin and this man! She felt she walked a tightrope and one false move would be sufficient to ruin everything.

'And have you missed me, Valerie?'

'Of course,' she replied, struggling to control her voice, to maintain normality in her tones.

'Have you seen Marco recently, *cara mia*?'

'Not for some time!' She held her breath, hoping the reply was correct.

A satisfied smile crept across Francesco's mouth.

'I'm pleased to hear that, Valerie. As you know, I cannot approve of my brother's behaviour ... His betrothal—' the old-fashioned word sat oddly between them—

'forbids that he should flirt so outrageously with you without arousing stormy emotions.'

Rayne contented herself with a smile. This was getting no nearer finding Valerie and, for a few moments, she was almost tempted to throw herself on this man's mercy. Perhaps he would help her to obtain a lead towards her cousin's whereabouts.

'So now, *cara,*' he went on, 'I wonder what plans you have for returning to England?'

Rayne's mind worked quickly. By the sound of it Valerie had mentioned the possibility of going home.

'Nothing is fixed,' she replied, 'but I think I must make a move shortly.'

'Back to see your cousin once more, yes?'

'Yes.' Rayne's breath came with difficulty.

'She will be pleased to see you, *si*?'

'Of course.' Why was he questioning her so closely? Had she inadvertently given herself away to him?

'It is good when family members live in affection and harmony,' he remarked, apropos of nothing, his eyes gazing past her at the flowering bushes which filled the night air with a mixture of heady scents.

She did not respond and the silence lengthened uncomfortably.

'Now if you will excuse me, Francesco,' she said at last, first to break the encircling quiet. 'I think I will leave you. I really do have rather a headache.' *And that was about the first totally honest thing she'd said this evening,* she silently added.

He accepted her words with a speculative glance and nod of the head.

'Did you travel here with Barbara?' he enquired courteously, taking her arm and leading her back towards the French doors.

'No, I came by taxi,' she said. 'I hoped I might be able to telephone from here to—'

He raised a remonstrative hand to stop the flow of her words.

'Giovanni will drive you back to your destination,' he said and, turning aside, he spoke in swift Italian to one of the servants. His instructions given he returned his attention to Rayne as he moved towards the entrance with her. 'It has been good to see you again, *carissima.* I shall hope to see you before you return to England.'

A uniformed driver stood waiting beside the well-polished limousine and Rayne guessed this must be the unknown Giovanni. He held the car door open for her and Francesco lightly kissed her hand before releasing his grip on it.

She got in and the car door closed. Giovanni took his place behind the wheel. Rayne gave him the name of the hotel and at last felt she could breathe properly. The evening had, of course, been a washout. She was no nearer finding Valerie than she had been when she had first arrived in Lugano. She felt foolish in her own eyes; she had been too ready to dramatise the situation.

The car sped swiftly back towards the Hotel Bon Accord and she was grateful for the driver's silent concentration on the road ahead. It gave her an opportunity to release the tension which the evening's masquerade had built up.

The hotel came into sight and Rayne felt sorry the journey had not taken longer. Her mind, however, was made up. She would return to London as soon as she could make a reservation on a London flight. She felt regret that she had not traced Valerie and enjoyed a few days in her company but—

The limousine drew up before the Hotel Bon Accord and the driver opened the door for her to alight and, as soon as she was on the pavement, handed her the small basket of silken posies which he had taken from her when she had got in. With a brief salute he took his own seat behind the driving wheel and set off once more into the stream of traffic.

Rayne turned slowly, making her way towards the swing doors, glad to be back in the now familiar surroundings of the hotel. It was a relief not to have to guard her expressions from watchful eyes.

She felt slightly ridiculous in her Victorian costume as she walked into the reception hall but it was comparatively deserted at this hour and the receptionist who handed her the key to her room wore the blasé expression of one rarely surprised by the eccentric behaviour of the hotel guests.

She had just pressed the button to call the lift when she heard his voice from behind her.

'*Signorina . . . Missa Steyning . . .*'

She turned swiftly, aware that the lift had drawn smoothly to this floor and the doors were opening. What could he want? The lift would be summoned to another floor in a moment . . .

The thoughts raced through her even as he extended the basket of flowers to her.

'You left this on the desk, *Signorina.*' His smile was courteous but never reached his eyes.

She took the basket from him and thanked him, turning on her heels and entering the lift.

It was only as the lift started to ascend she noticed the small silver-wrapped box nestling in the cushion of flowers. Small and unobtrusive . . . dainty and intriguing . . . It had not been there when she had set out . . .

Rayne's heart beat rapidly. Who had placed this parcel in her basket? And why?

CHAPTER EIGHT

Had the desk clerk placed the box in the flower-basket before handing it to her? Rayne dismissed the idea. He could not have guessed that she would absent-mindedly have left it on the reception desk.

Could it have been the driver of the car who had taken the basket from her during the journey from Francesco's villa back to the hotel?

Was it possible that it was Francesco himself who had slipped it discreetly into the flowers unobserved by herself?

In fact it might have been any one of the many guests who had thronged the villa for, on several occasions, Rayne had felt herself pushed in the press of chattering visitors.

Eager to undo the mysterious parcel she hurried the length of the long corridor. Fumbling with repressed impatience she thrust the key into the lock and entered the room, her gaze sweeping around almost as if she expected to find Valerie waiting for her. This was an evening of surprises and who knew if—But she cast aside the muddled, illogical thoughts and, sitting on the bed, carefully withdrew the box from the nest of flowers.

For one moment she wondered if the unidentified object could possibly be a *bomb* ... Then she laughed at herself for having such an incredible idea! Who could possibly want to plant a bomb on her!

She chuckled aloud and started to unwrap the object, her curiosity mounting apace as she tore the silver paper away to reveal the white cardboard box.

Only now did she hesitate. There was a sense of apprehension and Rayne was suddenly

68

aware that she had stepped into a situation for which she had been totally unprepared. Her plans for a few days' relaxation with her cousin were widely adrift from the reality which surrounded her.

White tissue paper concealed the contents of the box and Rayne parted the folds of it with careless haste, eager to see what object would be revealed to her curious gaze. The delicate paper tore beneath her rough treatment and she forced herself to extra care as she pushed aside the final sheet which wrapped the item.

It was with a gasp of surprise that she withdrew from the box the fair-haired doll, dressed in Swiss national costume; each miniature garment sewn with neat precision, Rayne was charmed with the immaculate presentation. The white broderie anglaise blouse, the striped full-skirted pinafore slip encrusted with diamanté which sparkled iridescently in the electric light, the tiny boots, the little cap set on the blonde pigtails and the smiling features of the doll . . . It was beautiful.

The only thing which worried Rayne was that she had no idea why this charming novelty should have been given to her and—more worrying still—*who* had gone to such elaborate lengths to hide the doll in the recesses of her flower-basket.

She turned and twisted the doll about within her fingers, trying to puzzle the reason for the mysterious events which had been set in train.

Smuggling! There was a chill feeling down her spine as she remembered the numerous 'thrillers' she had read in which drugs had been concealed inside a doll in order to smuggle them through customs.

She felt vaguely stupid as she undressed the bibelot, searching for signs of a place in which a small item might be concealed. There was nothing and, short of actually breaking the doll in two, there was no way in which she could tell if there was anything inside it or not.

She regarded the object speculatively, but the exquisite features of the doll, each tiny detail in perfect proportion, rendered such an act of destruction impossible.

Rayne's feelings were in a tumult. How she wished she could meet Valerie. She was sure that her cousin held the key to understanding the many ramifications of the situation which had brought Rayne all the way from England.

She walked over to the window, looking out over the black waters of the lake; it was lit by a myriad reflections from the coloured lights which adorned the boats and a silver stream of moonlight cut across the smooth surface.

Along the promenade she could see several couples strolling, hand in hand. She guessed that a selection of music from the pavement cafés would be adding an enchantment to the night and, opening wide the window and stepping out on the balcony, she strained her ears to listen to the romantic notes of the

70

mandolins which would doubtless be serenading any who cared to listen. She was rewarded by hearing an unforgettable tenor voice singing a Neapolitan love song and felt her heart soaring with the music itself.

So carried away was she by the magical combination of the music, the night and the beauty she almost forgot the doll she had left on the bed. The puzzles she had met since her arrival had vanished into the background and, briefly, she lived only for the present moment. The past with its problems had faded and the future with its as yet unknown questions to be answered had not arrived.

As she stood on the balcony, the light breeze riffling her hair almost lovingly, she looked across to the wide promenade which skirted the lake. For a moment her eyes did not fully register the person who stood by the railings, apparently lost in contemplation of the Hotel Bon Accord. As soon as she realized the identity of the watcher, Rayne obeyed the impulse to cram the doll inside her handbag, snatch up a woolly jacket and go across to the lakeside.

Cursing the incongruity of her cumbersome nineteenth century gown, she hurried to the lift and made her way out of the hotel, ignoring the questioning glance of curiosity the receptionist cast her.

Hurrying across the road Rayne searched the lakeside with anxious eyes, fearing that the objective of her haste, might have already gone.

But no! Relieved to see the tall figure still there she moved towards him and touched the sleeve of his jacket to attract his attention.

CHAPTER NINE

'Dean! What are you doing here?'

Dean Kenton turned towards her with a smile which lit the dark features of his face. Rayne had the impression she had brought him back from a dark No-Man's Land of thought and she wondered what had caused the shadows in his eyes.

'Wondering if it was too late to come calling on you, if you must know,' he replied lightly. 'I saw the light come on in your room and was anxious to hear how you made out during this escapade.' He glanced down at her long gown and smiled sardonically. 'So you went as a product of the nineteenth century . . . Not really your style, Rayne.'

She regarded him sharply. 'Exactly what do you mean by that remark?' she demanded.

'I believe the women of that era were more compliant with their menfolk.'

'Rubbish! Women have always thought and acted for themselves. We simply make less secrecy about it now.'

Dean laughed, turning away and leaning his elbows on the rail overlooking the lake. His gaze ranged over the dark, oily sheen of the water which contained the darker reflections of the surrounding mountains in its silky depths. 'I'll believe you if all women are like you.'

He spoke jestingly but Rayne was aware of a seriousness underlying his tones. She sensed that there was something bothering him and was at a loss to understand that her own problems could disturb him to such a degree. She suddenly felt shut out and resented it.

'Meaning . . .?' She glared angrily at him, the moonlight making her eyes glitter like stars in the oval of her features.

'I never met such an obstinate female before.'

'Then you must have led a peculiarly sheltered life.'

'I wouldn't have thought so.' He paused, then added: 'But none of this is getting us anywhere. Did you learn anything this evening which might help to give you a lead towards finding Valerie?'

For a split second Rayne hesitated, wondering how much to confide in this man. Why was he taking such an interest in her affairs? After all, were they not merely holiday acquaintances who had chanced to meet on a journey and, for companionship's sake, met again for a meal? Why had he been watching her hotel as if maintaining surveillance on her?

As swiftly the sense of distrust vanished. Perhaps it was only natural that he should want to know that she had finally made contact with Valerie after her confidences. Curiosity is a hungry animal and satisfaction important.

'No, nothing specific,' she said slowly, 'but—' she paused and he turned his gaze from the lake back to her, meeting her eyes levelly as he waited for her to continue—'something rather odd has happened.'

His mouth quirked for a moment but, as if he repressed the urge to smile, he controlled it in a firm line. 'I should have thought rather a lot that's odd has been happening. I admire your gift for understatement when you refer to "something" odd.'

She smiled obliquely at him. 'I suppose you're right, Dean. All right! Something *else* rather odd has happened.'

She halted as once again she puzzled as to how the doll could have been placed inside the basket of imitation flowers without her knowledge. Dean Kenton remained silent as if unwilling to intrude his presence into her train of thought. She was grateful to him for his patience and suddenly glad that she had somebody here in whom she could confide. The words began to spill out as she related the evening's events to him. He listened patiently while she told him of the conversation she had had with Francesco and tried to describe the house and other guests.

It was only when she reached the part of her story where Giovanni had driven her back to the hotel that she found her voice faltering. She knew Dean had noticed the strained manner which affected her and the expression of curiosity in his eyes deepened. She hesitated a moment as if seeking the right words.

'Now we come to the odd incident?' he prompted her.

She nodded. 'When I—I reached my room,' she said, 'I looked in my flower-basket . . . Oh! I went to the party dressed as a Victorian flower-seller,' she added in response to the puzzled frown which momentarily flickered across Dean's features. 'I forgot to tell you that Francesco had given instructions as to what I should wear. Anyway, when I got back to the hotel I saw that, hidden in the flowers, was a box which contained a doll. I simply don't know how it could have got there.'

'A *doll* . . . ?' he repeated. 'What have you done with it? You'd better let me have it at once. I believe you're getting involved in matters which are taking you out of your depths.'

Rayne felt her indignation rising in response to his statement. Did he think she was helpless . . . brainless? The surge of anger subsided in the relief of having confided the happenings to another human being. There was a lot of truth in the old adage about a trouble shared, she decided. She controlled the first sharp retort which had sprung to her lips but, still unwilling wholly to trust Dean, she shook her head.

'I—I want to keep the doll for a time,' she

said hesitantly. 'There must be a reason for it being placed in my possession and I'm certain that it has something to do with Valerie.' She paused before adding: 'Even if I don't know exactly *what*.'

'And while you're waiting to find out we may be losing the opportunity to trace the doll to its source,' Dean said, his tone reasonable and controlled.

Rayne sensed a repressed anger but, determined not to hand over the doll, her hand involuntarily tightened on the clasp of her handbag, almost as if she were afraid he might try to wrest it from her. Unwilling to meet the steely eyes which bored down into her features, she turned to look back at the white edifice of the Hotel Bon Accord across the wide avenue. Here and there a few lights still gleamed in the bedrooms of late revellers but the entrance hall provided a bright lake of golden light and made a focal point in the darkness of the night.

Rayne's gaze swiftly ranged the front of the building, pausing momentarily at her own window. For a moment—But no! There was no light to be seen now. And yet . . . there it was again . . . That slight movement . . . a flicker in the background . . . a shadow . . .

She strained her eyes but the impression of fleeting variations in the light had vanished. She imagined that it must have been the reflection caused by one or other of the tiny craft festooned with strings of coloured lights, moving swiftly across the lake, returning to its night-time berth. There were few tourists about now and, glancing at her watch, Rayne gasped with horror at the hour.

'Look at the time!' she exclaimed. 'I had no idea it was so late.'

Dean's frown deepened. 'Don't try to change the subject! We were talking about that doll. You must give it to me, Rayne. Let me deal with the matter.'

His pressure intensified her unwillingness to hand over the small object which was the centre of the argument.

'Perhaps tomorrow,' she said hesitantly, deciding that compromise might be the better way of dealing with Dean's insistence.

'Why procrastinate? Surely you can see this entire situation is getting out of hand?'

'I don't have the doll with me,' she lied, 'and I'm tired, Dean. I want to go back to the hotel and get a few hours' sleep. We'll meet again tomorrow, shall we?'

She could see the reluctance in his eyes and knew that he was about to offer more argument. Unwilling to face further confrontation she started to walk away. He flung out a hand, caught her wrist and turned her back to face him once again.

'You are probably the most confoundedly independent female I've ever met,' he said softly, still grasping her arm in a grip which bit into her flesh. 'Be careful that you don't live to regret your own independence, Rayne.'

Abruptly he released her and quickly she started to walk away from him before he could delay her once again. His words contained a note of threat and she gave an involuntary shiver of apprehension. What was Dean's interest in the affair? He seemed to have involved himself far more deeply than their brief acquaintanceship warranted.

Once again she recalled how, on their first meeting, he had called Valerie by name and, Rayne was as sure as she could be, that she had not mentioned her cousin by Christian name.

Tremors of something akin to fear yet not so definite moved on the nape of her neck. She wanted to reach the sanctuary of her hotel bedroom; there the anonymity would offer her a brief respite and give her the opportunity to collect her thoughts together. She had told Dean she was tired but sleep had never felt further away than it did at this moment. Every nerve in her body was alert to the unseen dangers which menaced her on all sides.

And even as the realization of her fears and thoughts struck her with force, Rayne laughed at herself for dramatising the situation beyond all belief. She was becoming neurotic, she told herself firmly. The best thing she could do would be to sleep for an hour or two and then, first thing in the morning, she would make arrangements to return to England. Let Valerie contact her there and—Rayne's lips tightened!—her cousin had better have a good explanation for all the upheaval she had been responsible for causing.

And Dean? Rayne was very conscious of the doll in the handbag. Should she give the cause of all this argument to Dean before she left?

Questions ... questions ... They pursued Rayne on all sides as she made her way into the foyer of the hotel. She had half expected that Dean would follow her across the wide avenue to the entrance but, turning there to look back over her shoulder, she realized he had made no attempt to do so. She felt an instant sense of let-down, and then chided herself for the perversity in her own nature which rendered her disappointed that he had not done so.

He was still resting his arms on the lakeside railing as he gazed out over the smooth silk of the lake but, as if feeling her eyes watching him, he turned to glance over at her. Even from this distance, although unable to make out the expression on his features, she felt their eyes meet, and was aware of a tiny shock of contact as their gazes interlocked. For one moment she hesitated, wondering if she should retrace her steps and hand over the doll into his keeping. She felt an almost desperate need to relieve herself of the responsibility which weighed so heavily upon her. But, as if he dismissed her with a careless shrug, Dean raised a hand in casual farewell and returned his attention to some distant point across the lake. The abrupt removal of his attention was the deciding factor. Rayne's lips tightened into an obstinate line and she made her way into the hotel, wondering what Dean found so engrossing in the darkness of the night and the restricted vision it offered. It seemed it must be the secret world of his own thoughts which held him enthralled.

Collecting her key she made her way into the lift and up to her room.

As soon as she opened the door and crossed the threshold she was aware that a stranger had been in here during her absence. She did not know herself exactly how she could be so certain but, as she switched on the lamp, she knew that her privacy had been invaded just as surely as she knew there was a gathering menace in this entire situation.

Glancing around she was relieved to see that everything appeared to be normal. Perhaps she was mistaken in this feeling that another presence had been in here. She began to breathe more easily, closing the door behind her and making her way towards the balcony where she intended to see if Dean was still standing where she had left him.

It was only as she did so that she saw the tiny signs which confirmed those first swift impressions. A drawer not quite closed ... Rayne knew that she had not left it like that. The door leading into the adjoining bathroom was ajar ... It had been shut when she had left.

80

The wardrobe door was also off the latch . . .

It was too late for any of the hotel staff to have come to her room for any reason. Much earlier in the evening the chambermaid had already turned back the bedclothes.

No, somebody had been in here searching amongst her belongings. Rayne shuddered. Surely there could be only one reason for this interest. Somebody was looking for the doll . . .

CHAPTER TEN

Rayne opened her handbag to check that the doll was still safely hidden away within its depths. The action was a reflex need to ensure that it was in her possession since there was no way in which it could have been removed without her knowledge.

It seemed to her that she had been given a vital clue to the mystery which surrounded Valerie. The only trouble was that she could not fathom its secret.

Somehow this charming little doll—Rayne took it out, carefully examining it again— concealed answers to questions which troubled Rayne at this moment and yet she was too—too *dumb,* she told herself angrily, to see the true significance.

Dean? Was he still standing beside the lake? She hurried over to the French windows leading to the balcony beyond and, opening them wide, stepped out into the warm night air.

The wide promenade circling the lake was empty and she felt the sudden surge of hope which had filled her slowly evaporate away.

There was little sleep for Rayne that night. She scarcely closed her eyes and yet, in some strange way, she welcomed the hours as and opportunity to assemble her thoughts into an orderly sequence. From the jumble of emotions which plagued her she extracted only the main details over which to mull; like an aching tooth, she felt the same need to explore the situation again and again as if some new light might suddenly be thrown on it revealing the answer which had previously been concealed from her.

The telephone call from Dean came early— just as Rayne, without the need of words, had known that it would. She had showered and dressed soon after seven o'clock and, after two cups of coffee and a *brioche* in the hotel dining-room, she had received the message that a gentleman wished to speak with her on the telephone.

She had hurried towards the line of four telephone cubicles in the main hall, making her way towards the end one where the hall porter indicated. Heart beating swiftly and the palms of her hands clammy, she realized at that moment how vulnerable and alone she really felt.

'Dean? Is that you?' Her voice was a shade higher than usual and she coughed slightly to conceal the transparent nerves which gripped her.

'Who else?' he quipped, sounding almost light-hearted.

She recognized his voice at once and relief flooded her being. For one moment as she had lifted the receiver she had wondered if— Abruptly she pulled her attention back to the business in hand.

'Dean, I must see you . . . as soon as possible,' she added.

'Why? What's happened?'

She heard the sharpening of interest in his tones as if his thoughts had been absent-mindedly straying to other—and more agreeable—matters.

'I—I'd rather not explain over the phone,' she said. 'Can you meet me?'

There was an almost imperceptible hesitation, then: 'I have an appointment at nine o'clock,' he said. 'I reckon I shall be about an hour. Will you meet me outside the *Cattedrale di San Lorenzo* at ten?'

'Yes, all right.'

'You know how to get there?'

'I'll find my way.'

'You could take the funicular up the hill.'

'I've told you . . . I'll find my way. I'm not an idiot.'

'No?' There was a question in the monosyllable. Then: 'Are you intending to bring that doll with you?'

83

Again she felt the icy fingers on the nape of her neck but, she suddenly realized with a chilling sense of acceptance, she had to take a chance on trusting somebody and Dean Kenton was the most prepossessing candidate to receive her confidences. At least she knew for certain that he could not have been the guilty culprit who had entered her bedroom searching—for what? ... the doll?—the previous evening since they had been together during those vital minutes. The silence became protracted; she could feel it lengthening, becoming heavy, almost as if it were a tangible entity.

'Well?' he prompted her impatiently. 'Are you bringing it?'

'Yes,' she answered.

'Right. See you later. 'Bye for now.'

'Goodbye.'

The time dragged until she deemed she might start out to meet Dean. She set off early, walking slowly through the arcaded streets of the town until she came to the hill which led to the magnificent Cathedral. Slowly she made her way up, past the small shops, many containing the wide variety of goods designed to catch the attention of the tourist. But this morning Rayne had no eyes for the colourful displays; all her thoughts were concentrated on her imminent meeting with Dean and the doll she had placed inside her handbag.

Arriving at last at her destination she walked

into the small *piazza*, admiring the carved doors of the *Cattedrale di San Lorenzo*, an outstanding feature of its design and architecture. She was alone in the square, an air of solitude cast a welcome tranquillity over the atmosphere and she made her way to the wall overlooking the roofs and town below. The sun was warm on her head and she lifted up her face to its rays, breathing deeply and feeling the tension and agitation recede into the background of her thoughts.

She knew that she was early for her rendezvous with Dean and was glad for these few moments of respite in which to relax and assemble her jumbled emotions into a semblance of order. A party of laughing, noisy Americans crossed the *piazza* almost within touching distance of her hand and one brash man amongst them cast her a flirtatious, inviting smile. She returned it coolly and then let her gaze slip from him, focusing once more on the pink and green tiles of the roofs below her. She sensed a momentary disappointment emanate from the stranger and was aware of a feeling of relief as the group moved out of her orbit and out of earshot. She wanted no distractions to the thoughts which obsessed her waking moments and the concern for her cousin which mounted steadily, filling her being with a sense of urgency she could not explain.

'Hello! I hope you haven't been waiting long.'

Dean's voice cut into her thoughts, startling

85

her from the reverie into which she had fallen. She wheeled smartly around, trying to conceal the panic which had inexplicably risen within her at the appearance of this man. *Friend?—or enemy?* At this moment she still did not know. Rayne could not pretend that his interest in her was innocent; somehow she was convinced that he was more deeply involved than he would have her believe. Desperation had forced her to trust him and she could only hope that her confidence would not be misplaced.

'Hello! No, I've only been here a few minutes myself. I found it rather pleasant just to ... to catch my breath in a manner of speaking.'

He smiled cursorily, extending his hand as if impatient for her to give him the doll. His abrupt manner sent that warning thrill snaking down her spine once more, but she felt she had no alternative other than to extract the object of so much interest from her bag and place it in his waiting grasp. Even as she took it out she regarded him with a waiting, wary expression in her eyes. He looked at her, sensing her close scrutiny then, as if guessing the secret doubts and fears which gripped her, his face lightened and he laughed in amusement, his gaze meeting her own with a jovial and open honesty which put her suspicions to flight.

'So you still don't completely trust me, Rayne?' His tone was kindly and there was no reproach in his eyes despite his words.

86

'There is so much I don't understand,' she answered, speaking slowly, feeling a need to answer with a frankness which met his own. 'Why are you so interested in my—my problems? I can't understand it. We were simply two strangers who shared an aeroplane flight together and—and yet now you seem to have taken as much trouble as if—as if—' She broke off, not knowing how to continue the muddled sentence, her emotions so chaotic that she could not assemble her thoughts into coherence.

'You can't understand why I should be interested in *you*?'

There was a teasing expression on his face. Rayne lowered her eyes, feeling oddly foolish beneath his mocking gaze. The doll she held within her hand was forgotten now. He waited for her to speak and, for a second, she hesitated, knowing she must control her breathing before she could trust her voice to answer him. She lost account of time as she fought for her self-composure and, to her mounting alarm, Dean leaned forward, stroking her cheek with a gentle hand.

'That's not what I said.' She jerked her head away from his touch, wondering at the rate of her pulse-beat, fighting to show an unruffled calm which would perhaps instil reality into this strangely dreamlike scene. 'I said you were showing an undue interest in my problems . . . I can't help wondering why!'

87

'Perhaps because I want to share *everything* with you—the good and the bad. Hadn't you considered that explanation?'

'No. Please, Dean, let's be serious, shall we? I'm not here to amuse myself with idle flirtations. I'm here to find Valerie and, if you can't help me, I don't want to waste my time like this.'

'I wonder why it's always an "idle flirtation" . . .?' Dean spoke contemplatively, reaching out his hand and taking the doll from Rayne. 'It seems to me there's nothing much "idle" about it—more like hard work!'

She watched him as he carefully examined the doll, aware that his words were merely a cover for the precise and detailed scrutiny which he afforded the toy. The delicate item looked incongruous in his strong hand and Rayne felt her attention riveted on the tanned fingers which turned it this way and that on his palm before Dean deposited it in the pocket of his jacket and threw a sunny smile in her direction. It was as if he had suddenly lost interest in the doll and dismissed the entire incident from his mind. She felt a sense of shock at his indifference to the object which had caused her such anxiety.

'Well? What do you think?' she demanded eagerly. 'What reason could there have been for somebody to plant that doll in the basket of flowers?'

Dean paused a moment, then: 'I can't

answer that question immediately, Rayne,' he said, 'but as soon as I know, I'll tell you.'

She cast him a questioning glance. 'You sound as if you're determined to find the answer to this puzzle yourself.'

He smiled down at her. 'Why not? You've intrigued me with all this mystery.'

She was not satisfied with his explanation. His interest went far beyond the bounds of human curiosity. She knew there would be little to be gained by questioning him any further; he was not the type of man to disclose any more than he intended and it was clear from the shuttered expression in his eyes that he had already said all he meant to on the subject.

'Well—'she hesitated awkwardly for a moment, 'I'd better get back to the hotel now.'

Unexpectedly Dean reached forward as she started to move away, he caught her hand in his and drew her back towards him, so close she could feel his breath warm on her cheek. Surprised, she tried to pull free, but he resisted her involuntary move and, against her will, she found herself enclosed within the circle of his arms.

She tried to protest but, even as she went to speak, Dean's lips closed over hers, pressing bruisingly down and trapping her mouth beneath his own. Struggle as she might she knew she could offer no strength to countermatch his. The realization afforded her a temporary pause in her efforts to resist and, to her amazement and as if they acted on their own volition, her arms moved about his neck. A thrill passed through her body and she felt thought take flight, was aware only of the sense of drowning in the power of this unexpected, undreamed of moment. As if Dean carried her with him on the crest of his ardour, she was unable to make any further move to remove herself from the circle of his arms. Unexpectedly she was aware that she had been travelling inexorably towards this moment, had known from the beginning that Dean had touched chords within her which had never been touched before. Had she been fool enough to fall in love with him? The idea hit her like a blow. Had she? *Had she?* The question beat at her even as her lips clung to Dean's and their bodies pressed close, close together.

Thrill-filled and powerless to resist it was as if she suddenly stood aside and watched these events with a stranger's eyes. Horror engulfed her, pushing aside her warm response to Dean's passion. As if imbued with extra force and strength by the question which she refused to answer even in the depths of her own subconscious mind, she pulled herself free. White-faced and angry-eyed she stood and regarded him while she fought to regain control over her errant emotions, hesitating to speak because she feared that her voice would give away her perturbation. Dean watched her, scrutinizing each changing expression of her face. She was aware of his watchfulness and, unable to meet the level regard, she lowered her gaze and, struggling desperately to control any giveaway tremor in her voice, she broke the pregnant silence which hung so heavily between them.

'You really are the most conceited man I've ever had the misfortune to meet,' she said coldly. 'I warn you that you'd better not try to do that ever again. Not that you'll have much chance. I'm going back to England on the first flight I can get and I sincerely hope I never meet you again.'

And turning sharply on her heels, Rayne made her way as quickly as she could out of this peaceful *piazza* towards the narrow street which led back to the town and lake. Her ramrod back and uptilted chin were evidence of her anger.

But Dean could not see the inner turmoil of her thoughts and emotions. Especially the emotions.

CHAPTER ELEVEN

Rayne's mind was made up. As soon as she reached the hotel she would phone the airline and arrange her return flight. Complications seemed to abound all the time she remained here; the place itself might be idyllic but her particular situation was far from that state.

Her feet traversed the pavements with speed but it was impossible to escape the wild tumult of her thoughts and the feelings which set her heart racing within her. Dean's kiss had surprised her in its warmth and intensity, but what had surprised her more was her own response to his touch. Never before had she known such a complete abandonment of identity in the circle of a man's arms and Rayne had no wish to surrender herself so weakly to the power he apparently wielded over her.

Power? *Was it power?* she questioned herself as she hurried along the narrow streets, oblivious to all the sights and scenes about her as she battled to control the errant confusion which ranged her being. Power was a word which seemed to suggest an outside influence over her instead of that inner, racing storm which sent her heart beating as if she had run a marathon. And *why*, for a few seconds, had she allowed herself to forget that she was here to look for Valerie? For a brief moment she had let herself relax in the embrace which had offered momentary escape from the problems which abounded on all sides. Why, too, did she still feel a speeding of her pulse when she remembered the comfort Dean's arms had contained and the promise of his kiss?

Love was a strange companion to have encountered during this so-called vacation!

Rayne halted in her tracks, almost tripping up the black-clad Italian woman following close on her heels. She muttered an apology which was received with an irritated scowl and a cursory nod. Then, more slowly now, Rayne set off once again, making her way towards the lakeside and the hotel.

Love!

The word had astonished her out of the welter of emotions which gripped her. Love? Had she been foolish enough to allow herself to fall in love with Dean during this short break in her routine? Of course not, she told herself staunchly. Such an idea was ludicrous; all her thoughts and ambitions had been centred around Valerie and the need to find her as soon as possible.

There had been little opportunity to consider her own feelings or where they might be leading her. It was only now she thought about the inexplicable strength she had drawn from Dean's nearness to her, the relief she had experienced each time he had assured her of his support, if not with words then just by his presence. Was that sense of comfort brought about by *love*?

Angrily she refuted it, unwilling to concede that she could have let herself be trapped by emotions even while her attention was ostensibly given to Valerie and the problem of her unexplainable disappearance. The one certain fact to which she clung, as a drowning man clings to driftwood, was that she must leave Lugano as soon as possible.

As if her decision impelled her feet to

greater speed, she increased her pace.

The lakeside was teeming with tourists meandering along and taking visible enjoyment in the busy water-traffic which filled the sparkling waters of the lake. Colourful sails and small power-boats; water-skiers and flag bedecked tourist excursion boats; reflections of the surrounding mountains in the blue surface of the water. All combined together to form a tapestry of colour, a ballet of life and movement which provided the onlooker with an inward joy and satisfaction which went beyond description. But Rayne strode along heedless of her surroundings.

The hotel was looming into sight now and she hastened her step, intent only on making the telephone call which would be her first act when she entered inside.

But it was not to be.

Collecting her room key at the desk, she took the lift to her floor, meaning to phone from the privacy of her room. No sooner had she entered the room, however, than the low-pitched burr of the bedside telephone board summoned her.

'*Pronto!*'

'*Pronto, Signorina.* There is a telephone call for you. A *Signorina Palmer.* I put-a you through, *si?*'

Valerie! Like a bolt from the sky the name of her cousin hit Rayne with almost physical violence, sending thought flying and stunning

94

her into a momentary sense of disbelief. Gathering herself together she made a deliberate effort to control the trembling of her hands and the giveaway tremor of her voice as she spoke.

'Thank you. Yes, please put the call through.'

There was a brief pause. Then: 'Rayne! Hello, how are you? Enjoying your holiday in Lugano?'

It really was Valerie. At last! Rayne had half expected to hear a stranger's voice, but there was no doubt in her mind that it was really her cousin at the other end of the line. Relief flooded through her in wave after wave before astonishment at Valerie's casual manner filled her and she could not completely conceal the note of irritation which fired through her.

'I don't know about "enjoying" my holiday, Valerie. I've been so anxious about you. Where on earth have you been? What's wrong?'

'Why should there be anything wrong? Surely I'm free to take off for a day or two if I wish, Rayne. You're not setting up as my keeper, are you?'

Rayne gritted her teeth, struggling to quell the swift rise of anger.

'Since you invited me to come out here to spend a few days with you I merely assumed you'd have the courtesy to let me know if you changed your plans, Val. But it's not quite as simple and uncomplicated as you make it sound. Why does this hotel have no record of you ever having stayed here? And who was that so-called friend of yours who telephoned me in England and ordered me not to come out here?'

'It's a long story, Rayne.'

'I've plenty of time to listen. You caught me just before I was going to book a flight home.'

'I'd like to see you before you go back to England.'

'Not as much as I'd like to see you,' responded Rayne drily.

'There's quite a lot to talk about.'

'Then might it not be a good idea to talk?'

'It's a little difficult for me to get away.'

Rayne's brows drew together in puzzlement. 'Where are you?'

'I can't tell you over the telephone.'

'Valerie, what's going on? For goodness' sake, explain what all this cloak and dagger business is about. Are you all right?'

'Yes, of course I'm all right. Why shouldn't I be? Do you think I can't take care of myself? I'm fine!'

Rayne detected a defiance in her cousin's tone which did little to allay her qualms. Surely she was protesting too much that all was well! She feared that her headstrong cousin was in a predicament which she was unable to handle satisfactorily and Rayne was conscious of her anxiety rising to the surface once again, driving out the irritation she felt at Valerie's strange behaviour. There had always been this wild

96

streak in her nature; even when they were children Rayne had been aware that there was a weakness in Valerie's character which allowed her to be easily misled.

The premonition that all was far from well was gradually strengthening and Rayne felt she was stepping out on an untried ground full of pitfalls to trap her. Each word she uttered must be carefully considered if she were not to lose Valerie's confidence. She prayed for wisdom, hoping that she would not frighten her cousin off. At least Valerie *had* contacted her at last. She was apparently in good health and a free agent despite all Rayne's secret anxieties.

'Are you in Lugano?'

'Near.'

'Where exactly?'

'I'm staying with a friend.'

'That's no answer.'

'I can't tell you the address over the phone.'

'Why not?'

'You *do* ask a lot of questions, Rayne.' Valerie sounded ruffled.

'That's because there are rather a lot of questions which need answers, Val.'

'Now is neither the time nor place.'

'It's the only time and place I have had since I arrived here—' she paused a moment, then added sharply—'at your request, I might remind you.'

'Oh, I'm sorry it's all been such a muddle, Rayne, but, honestly, you must have been

97

enjoying your stay. Nobody could possibly come to Lugano and not love the place.'

'If their mind is preoccupied with other trifling matters, like one's cousin mysteriously disappearing off the face of the map, without any warning, I doubt that even Lugano has the power to captivate the visitor.'

'You're being horrid to me,' Val said petulantly. 'It's a pity you came if you feel that way.'

'Well, as I've already said, I *am* going to book a flight home. This conversation doesn't seem to be getting us anywhere.'

Rayne found her fingers tightly grasped around the telephone receiver, knew that every nerve in her body was alert and made a visible effort to relax the tension within her. From where she sat on the bed she could see Monte Generoso rising from the blue waters of Lake Lugano; the mountain wore a white collar of fluffy clouds around its neck and Rayne wondered briefly if the fine spell of weather was coming to an end.

'No. Rayne, you can't,' said Valerie urgently. 'Please don't go! I need to talk to you.'

'Well, can we meet somewhere?'

'Yes.'

'Will you come here?'

'No. Let's meet in a café somewhere.'

'All right. When and where?' The knuckles on Rayne's hands were white as she waited for Valerie to speak.

'Tonight. Let's say eight o'clock at the *Café Bellini*. Do you know it? It's a popular tourist spot on the lakeside near Castagnola.'

'Yes, I believe I passed it the other evening when I went to—' Rayne broke off, suddenly aware she might reveal too much and unwilling to lose the slight advantage she had gained with her cousin.

'It will be crowded at that time so we shall be less conspicuous and we'll be able to talk then.'

Again that thrill of fear touched the nape of Rayne's neck with icy fingers. Why this mysterious and secretive air? Why could they not meet this afternoon here in the Hotel Bon Accord? Why should they hide like criminals?

But even as the questions surged around Rayne's mind like a swarm of stinging bees, she knew there would be little to be gained by seeking an explanation at this moment for Valerie's incomprehensible behaviour. It was clear that there were a great deal of undercurrents to be discovered and Rayne felt herself momentarily dismayed by the situation.

She felt alone now as she had not felt herself alone since her arrival in Lugano. There was no way—nothing under the sun!—which would induce her to contact Dean Kenton after the events which had occurred this morning on the *piazza* in front of the San Lorenzo Cathedral. She felt herself strangely bereft of his support. She had not realized how much she had relied on him to boost her own flagging morale.

'Are you there, Rayne?'

Valerie's question broke into her troubled thoughts and she pulled herself sharply together.

'Y-yes. Sorry, Val! I was just—thinking.'

'Well, I'll see you at eight o'clock at *Bellini's*,' her cousin repeated. 'Until then, *ciao!*'

'*Ciao*, Valerie.'

Rayne replaced the receiver, feeling suddenly cold inside. Then she started to count the hours until she could set out to keep the rendezvous with her cousin. It was a long time to wait when every instinct in her body was urging her to action, when even her fingertips were tingling with a sense of anticipation.

CHAPTER TWELVE

Dressed in a navy dress with white collar and cuffs, looking neat and coolly businesslike, Rayne set out for her meeting with Valerie.

She had debated whether or not to take a taxi to the *Café Bellini*, but had finally deemed that to walk along the lakeside might at least serve to work off a little of the excess energy which filled her now that the hour of their confrontation was imminent.

How slowly the hours of the afternoon had passed! The see-saw of her thoughts had swung her between Dean Kenton and Valerie, each providing her with problems related and yet unrelated to each other. The 'If only' game had sent her thoughts winging in directions she would have preferred them not to go, and she welcomed the distraction this walk would offer.

The promenade was deserted at this hour. The tourists had temporarily forsworn the delights of the lakeside in exchange for dinner in their hotels and boarding-houses; soon they would return for the evening's diversions offered by the boat trips to the surrounding night spots and the pavement cafés where several hours' worth of entertainment could be enjoyed for the price of a cup of coffee or a glass of wine.

As Rayne strode along she could hear the mellow notes of a mandolin echoing plaintively across the water. She saw a small rowing boat bobbing gently on the surface and, strumming the musical instrument, a dark-skinned, olive-eyed youth, an air of dejection on his shoulders as if he would recall times long past in the music he played. He appeared oblivious of the few who might pause to listen to him; he was lost within the dark country of his secret thoughts.

The small tableau depressed Rayne for no reason she could explain; there was an air of sadness weighing her down. She would have expected to have felt an elation of spirit, an eager anticipation now that she was on her way to meet Valerie at last.

Making a positive effort to throw off the

temporary loss of morale she made her way swiftly towards Castagnola, way out of earshot of the solitary mandolin with its sweet but sad melody. Nearing the town cafés she heard the sounds of violins being tuned up; this was a town of music, love and laughter. There was no place here for this strange sense of loss which filled her being.

She was relieved to see the *Café Bellini* loom into view. She scanned the terrace of pavement tables and chairs in search of her cousin. There were only a few patrons at the tables at this hour; later they would be filled to overflowing.

Rayne had no difficulty in espying Valerie at a corner table and, pausing momentarily, she took a swift, sharp appraisal of her cousin's features, noting the wan complexion and the turned-down mouth, the air of anxiety which emanated from her.

Rayne shivered in sudden apprehension. What was wrong with Valerie? But even as she posed the question to herself, Valerie glanced up and met Rayne's scrutiny, her expression changing into a welcoming, carefree smile which held no hint of the earlier troubled preoccupation.

The deliberate alteration served only to accentuate Rayne's misgivings. Telling herself that she was allowing her imagination to run riot, she waved at Valerie as she threaded her way through the tables. For one wild moment she wished that she was back in London following her daily routine. She felt unprepared for this situation and almost feared what she might be about to hear. She chided herself for her own foolish trepidation and, looking down on Valerie's upturned, smiling face, she was aware only of a warmth of affection and relief flooding over her. Valerie was *safe*. She was *here*. At last they were united and all Rayne's nervous qualms were surely at an end.

'Valerie!' She greeted her with a note of welcome in her voice. Until this actual moment of meeting Rayne had secretly been afraid that it would not come to pass in spite of their plans. 'Thank goodness you're here.'

'Hello, Rayne. I'm sorry that—that things have been so difficult for you since your arrival in Switzerland.'

Rayne sat in the seat beside her cousin, placing her handbag on the table in front of her as the waiter came to take her order.

She asked for a coffee and then returned her attention to her cousin.

'Well, they've certainly been that one way and another!' she responded. 'I'm so glad to see you at last, Val, although—'a light of concern flickered in Rayne's clear eyes—'I have to say I don't think you look very well. Is there something wrong?'

'N-no.' The slight hesitation did not go entirely unobserved by Rayne but, before she could pursue the matter any further, her cousin spoke again, smiling as she said: 'I've had a few late nights and I don't think they altogether agree with me.' She took a sip or two from the cup of coffee on the table in front of her. Rayne felt it was a cover for her embarrassment.

'Have you been to parties like those given by your friend Francesco?' probed Rayne.

Valerie shot her a glance of astonishment. 'What do you know about him? You *must* have been doing your Sherlock Holmes act well!' The surprise in Valerie's eyes gave way to an almost spiteful expression before she wiped her face clear, deliberately forming her features into a bland, unreadable mask.

The snide remark caused Rayne a momentary sense of shock and she saw Valerie's careful control of her facial expressions. The momentary nakedness of her cousin's feelings did nothing to reassure Rayne that this situation owed much to her imagination.

'Put yourself in my place,' Rayne said sharply. 'It's not exactly pleasant to travel to another country to find the person you're supposed to be meeting hasn't even been heard of in the hotel in which she's supposed to be staying. Wasn't I *expected* to be anxious? Did you think I'd just go home the next day and wait until I heard from you? Use your loaf, Val!'

Valerie had the grace to look penitent, then: 'What's this about Francesco's party? Tell me how you came to meet him . . . to be invited to

104

one of his *soirées* . . .'

Half ashamed by her own temerity on reflection, Rayne told her cousin the events which had led up to the evening in question. She made no mention of Dean Kenton or the part he had played in all the happenings of the past few days; it was as if by carefully avoiding all reference to his name she could erase the memory of his kisses from her thoughts.

When Rayne came to speaking about the doll she had found in the flower-basket that night on her return to the hotel, she felt herself affronted at the expression of amused disbelief she glimpsed on Valerie's face.

'Why do you look like that?' she challenged her cousin sharply. 'I'm telling you the truth.'

'Of course you are,' soothed Valerie. 'I know *that*! But I think you're certainly reading too much mystery into it. Knowing Francesco as I do, it was simply a small souvenir of the evening. I expect all the guests received a similar memento of the occasion.'

Rayne swallowed hard. Had she over-reacted? It would not have been difficult in view of the happenings which had preceded finding the doll so carefully concealed in the basket. Suddenly she felt foolish, drained of all emotion—even curiosity.

'Where is it?' continued Valerie, not noticing the silence which constrained Rayne with unseen fetters. 'Do you have it with you?'

Rayne shook her head, more unwilling than

ever to reveal that she had handed over the doll into Dean's keeping. A glint of suspicion entered Valerie's eyes.

'You haven't taken it to the police or anything stupid like that, have you?' she demanded, angrily.

'Why should it matter if it's only a harmless souvenir?'

'Rayne—' there was a pause, then—'I've been a bit silly and not very truthful with you.'

Rayne felt a cold chill on her spine although the evening was warm, scented air from nearby linden trees wafting on the breeze.

'Then perhaps you had better start being truthful with me now.'

Unwilling to meet Rayne's eyes, Valerie fingered the spoon in her saucer, scrutinizing it as carefully as if it had a special meaning for her before she answered.

'I've been such a fool. I let myself fall in love with somebody and—' she blinked back a tear—'and when he knew I'd done so, he—he asked me to take a parcel of drugs through Customs for him. I refused and then he began to threaten me. Rayne,—' there was a note of desperation in Valerie's tone now—'I thought he was going to kill me. I telephoned you to come out here because I needed your help. I knew you wouldn't let me down.'

'But you weren't even staying at the Hotel Bon Accord yourself.'

'No. I intended to come there to see you

106

once you were booked in.'

'You've taken long enough contacting me. You must surely have realized how anxious I'd be about you.'

'Oh, Rayne, believe me, I'm sorry!' said Valerie, impassioned now as she reached across the table and grasped Rayne's hand in her own. 'After I telephoned you, a—a friend of mine offered me a hiding place at his villa in Como and I've been there. He told me he would phone you and tell you not to come out here. He would look after me without bothering you.'

'A charming way your friend has with him,' said Rayne drily. 'He made subtle threats as to what he would do if I dared to come to Lugano.'

Valerie looked astonished. Then: 'But you still came?'

'Of course.'

'Can you ever forgive me for landing you in this mess too? Rayne, I'm sorry!'

'What happens now? Will you come back to London with me?'

Valerie paled. 'No. I dare not. He'll—he'll kill me.'

'Who will kill you?'

'The man I told you about . . . the one I fell in love with.'

'Apparently it's true that there's no accounting for tastes!' Rayne returned sharply.

She felt utterly bewildered by her cousin's

107

garbled story, hardly able to credit all she was hearing. Was it perhaps some sort of practical joke? she wondered, but a glance at Valerie's distraught and worried face and she knew there was nothing even remotely humorous about this situation.

'You don't understand, Rayne. I don't want him to get into trouble and, if I can just hide out in Como for a while, I'll be able to return to England when the affair blows over. He won't be trying to find me *forever*... He *can't*... He'll have to go back himself sooner or later.'

'Don't be ridiculous, Val! I can't go back and leave you here in this situation. Are you crazy?'

'I'll be all right. My friend will look after me. But he does want you to go back.'

Rayne felt herself stiffen. 'The man you're staying with ... He knows I'm here?'

'Yes. He probably heard you were at Francesco's party and knew it wasn't *me* since I was with him that evening.'

'What a muddle! What a mess!'

'And all my fault,' added Valerie penitently. 'But I shall be all right now. Truly.'

'But I don't like to leave you here if this other man ... the one you're supposed to have fallen in love with ... is still about ... You may be in danger.'

'I think he will be going back to England himself soon. Then I'll follow and—Well, that'll be the end of the affair.'

'I should hardly think you'll be nursing a

broken heart over him.'

'You haven't met him, Rayne,' said Valerie softly. 'Dean's like no other man you've met before. He's—'

'*Who*? What name did you say . . .?' Rayne's voice was scarcely above a whisper. She waited in disbelief for her cousin to speak.

'Dean. His name is Dean Kenton and, honestly, Rayne, he's special. He's really special!'

CHAPTER THIRTEEN

Rayne's head was in a whirl. Returning to the Hotel Bon Accord she tried to settle her thoughts into a semblance of order. It was impossible. No matter how much she called logic to her aid, begged that common sense might dictate her next move, she was aware only of a desperate need to see Dean and demand confirmation of Valerie's astounding, incredible tale.

It was late when she and Valerie had finally parted company but, no matter how much Rayne had pressed her cousin for more details, she learned nothing which added further light on the situation.

Walking back now along the lakeside, Rayne wondered why she had not revealed her own acquaintanceship with Dean Kenton to her cousin. She was not normally secretive but, on this particular matter, discretion had sealed her lips on any confidences which she might have been tempted to disclose.

Was it that her own feelings were so closely involved with the object of her cousin's affections? Rayne was not sure what her motives for her silence signified. She only knew that now, as she strolled in the peaceful tranquillity of late evening along the Riva Vincenzo Vela, the rampant emotions which surged through her heart and being could no longer be denied.

No more could she pretend that the strange feelings which had possessed her when Dean had kissed her this morning—was it really only this morning?—were only the result of propinquity in this romantic atmosphere. Such reasoning could not account for the jealousy which had snaked through her as she listened to Valerie's revelations of her own love for the same man.

Rayne had never believed she was the jealous, possessive type. It had surprised her to feel the depth of pain which had surged into her being when she had heard Valerie speak Dean Kenton's name. She had had to grip her own hands tightly under the table in order to control herself from blurting out the fact that she herself had been foolish enough to let Dean throw a silken cord of love about her too. She felt as if she had inadvertently walked into a spider's web of deceit and intrigue; never in her wildest thoughts had Rayne ever reckoned to play a role in such an affair—mysterious dolls; drugs; hideaway villas in Como. It was all too much. Surely if she pinched herself she would wake up and find herself back in her small flat in London? Safe and secure from the situation in which she now found herself.

The line of lights crawling up the steep sides of San Salvatore marked the funicular railway; it beamed bright against the dark wooded slope. Haphazardly a myriad other lights sparkled on the mountain, looking like tiny stars which had spilled out of the heavens above.

A night breeze had sprung up riffling the leaves of the trees beneath which Rayne walked; it moved across the surface of the lake in a shimmer of iridescent light. The usual sounds of music and voices intermingling were gradually giving way to silence; it was a silence so tangible that it almost bore its own particular sound; there was a profundity in the atmosphere which settled on Rayne's spirit in an indescribable fashion.

She knew that she would never ever forget this night or the silent confessions she was making to herself about her love for Dean.

Yes. She would pretend to herself no longer. She had allowed herself to fall in love with Dean Kenton. For the first time in her life she had met a man who had called forth such a depth of response within her that she would have given all of herself into his keeping at this moment without pause or reservation.

And it had to be *him* . . .! Not only the man her cousin had fallen in love with but also a *crook* . . . Worse! A *drug-smuggler*, if Valerie was to be believed. To think how he had played with her—Rayne—during these past days.

Clearly he had hoped that she would lead him to Valerie's trail. Possibly he believed that she secretly knew Valerie's whereabouts and this was the reason for his undue interest in her. Perhaps this had been the reason for his kisses this morning! He had hoped that, by gaining physical domination over her emotions, she would reveal all she knew to him.

Rayne cringed inside herself. How well his attractions had worked on her! Even now in retrospect she felt the welling up of desire for his embrace engulf her. Bitterly, angrily, she fought against the longing she felt.

And how easily she had fallen a dupe to his cunning ploy!

Have I really been so gullible? she asked herself, anger rising within her. Have I really allowed myself to love a man who is so shamelessly dishonest . . . so rotten?

The words echoed around and around in her mind. She increased her pace in an effort to escape the taunting mockery of her own question. There was only one answer to it and, in supplying it, Rayne felt that she was submitting her own integrity into question.

There were few people about now on the shores of the lake. Rayne felt no nervousness though. Her attention was too preoccupied by the latest revelations to feel any qualms concerning her own safety. In fact, she added, it might almost be a mercy if some villain would knock me into unconsciousness! At least she would not then feel the ache which gripped her heart like a squeezed orange as she raced along in an attempt to escape her own pursuing thoughts.

Here and there beneath the canopy of trees a few couples strolled hand-in-hand, or sat on the wooden benches gazing into each other's eyes without need of words to intrude into their magic circle.

Rayne envied them all the very ordinariness of their lives. Why had *she* been picked on by an unkind fate? Why couldn't *she* just have met Dean Kenton and shared a happy, joyous relationship with him? Or—better still—never have met him at all! Never have come to Lugano . . . Never have allowed any of this magic to brush off on her . . .

She sighed. An elderly Italian gentleman turned to regard her curiously, believing she had been on the verge of speaking to him. Hastily Rayne averted her face, anxious not to have her thoughts interrupted by a stranger. The glint of hope in his eyes faded, giving way to a slightly aggrieved disappointment. He hesitated momentarily as if wondering whether

113

Rayne might offer him a sign of encouragement then, realizing that none was forthcoming, he continued to walk on, throwing only a glance of speculation over his shoulder.

Rayne had already forgotten him. He had scarcely penetrated the invisible wall she had built up around herself; a wall formed of the muddled confusion of her own thoughts and the worry about Valerie which still possessed her.

Although Valerie had done her best to assure her, Rayne could not still the gremlins of fear for her cousin. Admittedly she had now seen her for herself and Valerie was clearly a free agent or, otherwise, they would not have been able to meet on a café terrace. But why, *why* should this niggling anxiety still invade her thoughts?

Rayne began to feel as if she were in the grip of a fearsome nightmare which comprised all her deepest, most complex emotions.

Breathless with exertion she paused a moment, hand on the rail, looking out over the dark, oily-looking water of the lake; moonlight flecked the surface with diadems of light, moving, dancing, flickering, as the breeze gently stirred it.

Her eyes were deeply shadowed, her mouth set in a firm line as she struggled to come to terms with all the feelings which surged through her.

It was an impossible situation! The sooner she returned home the better. As soon as she was occupied once more with her work she would be able to put this strange time with all its associations behind her. There would be no time for dwelling on the past and wishfully daydreaming about Dean. He was a villain! A cunning rogue! Love could never be between them.

She heard a soft footfall approaching her and turned sharply, suddenly alert, her nerves tingling apprehensively.

The elderly Italian had decided to retrace his steps and was now drawing close to her. She realized that he had mistakenly assumed that she had stopped to admire the scenery as a pretext to encourage him! She resumed walking, her pace swift and determined, muttering imprecations beneath her breath on the subject of men in general. After a few moments she cast a glance over her shoulder, relieved to note that the importuning stranger had now stopped to survey the scenery himself. Innocent as the first snowdrop of spring he was engrossed in the magnificent spectacle of the sleeping, night-time lake. Rayne smiled grimly to herself and went on, her speed allowing for no misapprehensions should her follower turn to regard her again.

Within a few minutes the outlines of the Hotel Bon Accord were in sight. Unconsciously Rayne started to walk faster as if the hotel itself would offer a sanctuary to her. Unaware herself of the need she felt for a protection against the blows which fate had been striking, she believed that it was only the knowledge that as soon as she was back at the hotel she would be able to start making arrangements for her return home. Or first thing in the morning anyway! she added silently. She suddenly realized that, although it was late, she felt no trace of sleepiness; every nerve in her body was alert. She felt fresher than when she had set out to keep her rendezvous with Valerie. The adrenalin had flowed fast and furious and now she wondered how she would pass the remaining hours until morning. The one certain thing was that there would be no sleep for her this night.

She hurried up the steps leading to the hotel entrance, intent on reaching her room where she could reflect on the events of the evening in solitude. She wondered if room service would extend to a pot of coffee at this late hour and decided that there was no harm in asking.

The lights in the entrance hall were dimmed now and, as she pushed open the swing doors, and made her way through the entrance, she saw that there was only one yawning, sleepy-eyed night-porter on duty. He threw her a surly glance as if he resented her intrusion then, obviously recalling himself to his duty, he forced a half-hearted, polite smile of greeting.

She started to approach the desk to collect

her room-key but, before she could reach it, she felt her arm caught and held. She gave a tiny exclamation of startled surprise at the tall figure who towered over her. She had not observed the man get up from the deep armchair near the doorway, where he had been concealed, clearly waiting for her to return to the hotel.

CHAPTER FOURTEEN

'What the hell do you think you're playing at? How could you be such a bloody little fool as to be out alone at this time of night! And where the devil have you been anyway?'

The words flowed fast, furiously, as Dean Kenton's eyes met Rayne's in a level exchange. Anger sparked between them as if it were a live, electric-charge.

'What the hell has that to do with you? Who do you think you are? My bloody keeper . . .?' With an effort of control Rayne answered him quietly, coldly, through gritted teeth. She felt herself bridle, every nerve in her body tingling; she was consumed with a rage she had never before experienced. She longed to slap the face that loomed over hers, to express her frustration in physical violence.

Surprise flicked across Dean's face then, almost as if accepting her spirited right to defend her independence, he allowed his manner to relax. He smiled, a small smile that did not quite reach his eyes which still held the cold iciness of emeralds.

'I'm sorry, Rayne. I don't mean to intrude on your privacy. I'm merely concerned about you after the events of the past few days.'

'Then there's no need for you to concern yourself any longer.'

'Why? What's happened?' His questions shot out with the velocity of a bullet. With what seemed an almost involuntary gesture, his hand reached out, grasping her arm firmly.

Rayne cast a glance at the drowsy porter who appeared to be more alert now, studying them covertly as if sensing a drama being played out in the reception hall with only himself as onlooker. Seeing Rayne's awareness of him, he lowered his gaze and feigned interest in a sheaf of papers on the desk, shuffling hurriedly through them. Still she knew that his ears were alert to catch any word which might pass between Dean and herself and, since the porter's knowledge of English was not inconsiderable, she felt embarrassed by his presence.

'I—I can't talk to you here,' she said, casting a glance over at the desk. 'Can we go for a walk?'

'Of course. Let's go by the lake. We'll be alone there and—' a wry glance at his wristwatch and he added drily—'dawn is a very beautiful sight to watch as it creeps across the

118

water!'

'I didn't ask you to spend the night waiting for me,' she reminded him.

'I must admit I'd have preferred to spend it *with* you,' he said quietly.

She felt an urge to giggle at the expression on his face but she forced it back. She was unwilling to relax the anger which fired her. She needed to keep a barrier erected between them now more than at any time in their brief acquaintance. Not only was Dean an unknown quantity to her, a stranger who was displaying a more than normal interest in her welfare, but he was also the man whom her cousin had chosen to love. *What a cheap philanderer he must be! A womaniser of the first order!* Once again the adrenalin started to flow and Rayne defiantly tossed her head at him, quelling him with a cold glance of disapproval as she marched ahead of him out of the swing doors of the hotel.

In silence they walked across the wide road to the lakeside; it was not an unfriendly silence but Rayne felt it as an almost tangible entity between them. She tried to assemble her thoughts into a coherent form, rehearsing the words she would say when the moment for explanations was no longer possible to delay. It seemed to Rayne that the time for truth had arrived—but not about her own feelings for this man. Oh, no! That was a secret she would carry back to England with her—a secret she would guard for ever until the pain of loving

Dean had subsided into past memories. Only then would she be able to face the entire truth of her foolish surrender to his charisma.

'Well, Rayne! Where have you been?'

His words intruded almost harshly into her thoughts and, as she looked around her, she was surprised to see that they were both sitting on one of the wooden benches set beneath a giant magnolia tree; the enormous waxy flowers looked like large luminescent lanterns in the dark tracery of leaves above. She had been so preoccupied that she had not been aware of her surroundings until this moment.

Now the peace of the night encompassed them both like a cloak around their shoulders. Rayne felt almost afraid to breathe, unwilling to break the spell which had cast itself about them. The soft lap of the water against the stone wall and the shirring of the breeze through the branches overhead were the only sounds to disturb the silence.

She turned and eyed Dean reproachfully, resenting the intrusion of his importuning questions into the magic of the moment. As if intuitively sensing her reluctance to speak, he waited calmly, not showing his own inner impatience. He watched her steadily and she was aware of his regard although unable to read the thoughts flowing behind the bland, inscrutable mask he offered to her.

'I've been with Valerie. She's told me all about you.'

The blunt words slipped from her lips. She forced herself to look at Dean as she spoke, wondering if she would surprise some giveaway expression in his eyes. There was nothing. He did not speak. Rayne wondered if he had heard her properly and, running her tongue across lips gone suddenly dry, she said again: 'I've been with her all the evening and she's told me everything.'

A smile lurked for a moment on Dean's mouth before it fled, leaving the lips set in a stern line which bade no good to Rayne.

'*Everything . . .?* Now that sounds like a tall order! Suppose you tell me exactly what she told you in this heart-to-heart discussion you've shared.' His tone was mocking.

'Don't play games with me, Dean.' Rayne felt the slivers of anger stir once again.

'I don't think I'm the one who is playing. Tell me exactly what this charming cousin of yours has been telling you.'

'How can you speak like that about her! As if—as if you don't even like her . . .'

He gave a gentle laugh and reached out a hand to Rayne, taking hers and moving closer to her on the bench. She pulled her hand free from his and removed herself from his nearness, aware that she was now sitting on the end of the seat and there was no escape from him if he chose to move up again. He did not and she was aware of a tiny disappointment. She beat the traitorous feeling down, but felt strangely cold and unwanted.

'Don't let's become involved with emotions at the moment, Rayne. Let's stick to facts. Exactly what has Valerie been telling you this evening? Where did you see her?'

Rayne felt shut off from him, excluded now from that powerful magnetism which emanated from him. Clearly all he wanted to hear about was Valerie.

'She phoned me at the hotel and asked me to meet her at the *Café Bellini* this evening.'

'You should have called me. I would have come with you.'

'I don't need you to wet-nurse me, Dean. I'm perfectly capable of taking care of myself.'

'All right, Miss High and Mighty. Go on with your story.'

'Don't speak to me like that. I won't be patronized by you or—or—'

He held up his hands in a token of mock surrender. 'Sorry, sorry! Please continue and I promise not to interrupt again.'

'I fail to see why I should tell you anything. You already know.'

'I want to know exactly what she told you and where she is staying now.'

'Why? Are you afraid she told me too much?'

'What does that mean?'

'If you must know, she told me that you're involved with drug-smuggling and, in spite of that, she's in love with you—'

122

'*What . . .?*' Dean's face was a picture of total amazement. 'Drugs . . .? In love with me . . .? Do you actually believe such a load of nonsense?'

Rayne hesitated, shocked by his words. Then she remembered Valerie's expression when she had spoken of this man. Valerie was foolish and impulsive but she never lied. Of course she believed her cousin spoke the truth. The whole story was too far-fetched to be anything else than the stark truth. After all, Dean would scarcely be likely to *admit* to drug-smuggling and womanising anyway.

For the first time Rayne questioned her own wisdom in coming out on the deserted lakeside with this man. Perhaps she would have been more circumspect to have remained within sight of the hotel porter while she told Dean that she was familiar with his game and threatened to report him to the proper authorities if he ever came within a mile of her cousin again.

'Dean—' Rayne spoke quietly, trying to keep any note of fear out of her tones, 'I've known Valerie all my life and she wouldn't lie to me. Of course I believe her. But if you will promise me that you'll never try to contact her again I'll give you three days to get clear before I go to the police about the matter of the drugs you're involved with.'

'Why?' He eyed her questioningly. 'Why are you giving me time to make a getaway?'

'Because I—' Rayne broke off, feeling

123

wretched and unable to explain the wild contradiction of emotions which see-sawed her to and fro in a mass of indecisions and uncertainties. She started again, purposely controlling her tones: 'I just want to be finished with this whole unpleasant affair. I want to go back to England and forget you ever existed and I want Valerie to do the same. I want no reminders of you or this business in the shape of police courts and—and things like that. I just want never to see you again. I don't want even to *think* of you again.'

She was unaware herself of the tears which had escaped and were rolling down her cheeks like giant pearls. Dean Kenton reached out and brushed them from the smooth surface of her skin with a gentle forefinger. She tried to pull away from the insistent touch of his hand which seemed to burn through her being like a brand. She heard him give a soft laugh as he drew closer to her. She could not escape him; there was no escape anywhere from him.

His caressing hand moved from her cheek, pausing briefly on her breast as his lips moved forward to trap her mouth beneath his own in a bruising kiss. There was no tenderness in his touch as he pulled her into his arms and held her close against him. She could feel the thudding of his heart against her own and, for a crazy moment, her pulses raced as she strained her body against his, feeling the hardness of his muscles as their bodies ground one into the other in this crescendo of a passion which threatened to drown all common sense in its rising tide. His teeth caught her lips and she felt the pain of it, welcoming even that as, again and again, Dean's kisses melted the very essence of her being into a willing submission.

It was folly, *madness* . . . But a total commitment of her very soul to this man. She tasted the salt bitterness of her tears mingle with the sweetness of his kisses. A sob tore from her throat and was lost as Dean's voice murmured endearments against her ears, her throat, her mouth. She could not distinguish what he said but it did not matter. She was aware only of this consuming fire which burnt through her, the need for a physical fulfilment of the desire which racked her body in an overwhelming demand for this man's love. Never before had Rayne known this wild and unfettered passion. She had never imagined that her body could respond so eagerly to another's touch, had not fully realized the heights—or the depths—to which the touch of a certain man might lead her.

Suddenly reality confronted her, jerking her harshly back into the world about her, far from that place which only lovers can know and share. Rayne pulled herself free from Dean's arms, summoning all her strength to break from the circle of security which his embrace promised. False promises! False words! False kisses! Everything about this man was a sham and a lie.

Pain fired through her as she felt his arms go limp about her and she knew herself released from the spell which their shared ardour had cast over them.

'I'll never forgive you for that,' she murmured vehemently. 'Never!'

She got up from the seat, already moving away from Dean, even as she spoke. He hurried after her, calling her name but she pretended not to hear.

She was intent only on making her escape into the hotel. Once there she would pack her belongings together and make plans to leave Lugano at first light. If she could not get a seat on a plane back to England today she would fly anywhere in Europe. It didn't matter where as long as she put distance between herself and Dean Kenton.

CHAPTER FIFTEEN

As soon as she could, Rayne asked for her bill to be made ready. She was the first in the dining-room but coffee was all she ordered. She was unable to face food. Her heart felt too heavy within her and she was too full of the numerous arrangements she must make if she were to shake the dust of Lugano from her shoes this same day.

She made her telephone call to the airline office from the hotel bedroom, not wishing to make it from the public phones in the main hall where the holiday-makers would shortly be congregating to wait for the coaches which would call there to pick them up en route for the many tourist destinations.

Rayne was fortunate. There had been a cancellation on a flight from Zurich and, if she caught the next train there from Lugano railway station, she would be in time to take it.

She looked at her wrist-watch. She was making good time and, glancing at her suitcase, already packed and waiting, she decided she had time to take one last farewell of the lakeside which had so dominated her brief stay here.

A final glance around the room to make sure she had left nothing behind and Rayne turned on her heels to leave. She fought the sudden rise of tears to her eyes. Unexpectedly this moment of her final departure was causing her a pain she had not anticipated. That she had been foolish enough to allow herself to fall in love with a man she had known only so brief a time was bad enough, but that he was a rogue without morals of any sort was a double blow to the common sense she had believed herself to possess.

She paid her bill and, telling the porter she would be back shortly to collect her suitcase and order a taxi to the station, she made her way out of the hotel and over to the lakeside.

The air was refreshing and, looking around

her for this final farewell to a place which had captivated her with its magic, she felt unaccountably saddened by the knowledge that she would never again visit the *Ticino*.

Rayne was aware somewhere deep inside herself, that she would always associate Dean with these surroundings and, if she were to wipe his memory from her as if it had never been, then she must also forget Lugano and its ambience.

'*Buon giorno, Signorina. Come sta?*'

Rayne turned sharply to see who had addressed her and was surprised to see the elderly, grey-suited Don Juan who had tried to attract her attention the previous night. Not wanting to appear rude she murmured an acknowledgement to him and started to move away. She felt a momentary annoyance. She had wanted to bid a sentimental farewell to Lake Lugano in solitude. It seemed that even this small favour was to be denied to her.

'Excuse me, *Signorina* Stenning, may I speak with you one moment?'

She turned sharply, regarding this stranger with alert curiosity in her eyes.

'How do you know my name?' she demanded.

'I—' he paused, smiling charmingly— 'enquired at the Hotel Bon Accord this morning. After our—our little encounter yesterday, I found that I could not forget the *bellissima Inglese*.' His command of English was

128

excellent.

She felt annoyance rising. She had enough to bother her without the unwanted attentions of an elderly, flirtatious Italian.

'You had no right to do such a thing,' she snapped. 'Now if you will excuse me, I have a train to catch.'

She started to walk away but he caught her arm, holding it lightly.

'Please, you must forgive an old man who appreciates beauty . . . no matter in what form it comes. You are leaving Lugano?'

'Yes. Now, if you will excuse me,' she repeated, drawing her arm free. He made no move to stop her. 'I really must go if I am to catch the train.'

'Then I must wish you "Bon Voyage". I wish we had met much earlier.'

'Thank you. Goodbye, *Signore.*'

'*Ciao, Signorina* Stenning.'

He stood still. Rayne walked away, aware that he continued to watch her steadily, one arm on the railing which skirted the lake. She was acutely conscious of his gaze on her all the time she crossed the road. She was relieved to walk into the hotel and out of his view. She thought he meant no harm but she was in no mood for humouring lonely Italians who sought the companionship of young women!

She went straight over to the reception desk. The receptionist on duty greeted her with a smile and she asked if he would order her a taxi to take her to the railway station.

'*Si, Signorina, subito.* There is a parcel here for you, by the way.'

He reached under the long desk which ran the length of the hall and handed her a small box wrapped in a gift paper and tied with silver ribbons.

Rayne took it, a puzzled frown drawing her brows together in a deep furrow. There was no label on the parcel to indicate that it was intended for her.

'Are you sure this is for me? Who left it here?'

'*Si, Signorina,* it is for you. An elderly gentleman brought it in and enquired your name this morning. He left it for you and mentioned it would be a small souvenir of your holiday.'

But she had only just left him and he had made no mention of leaving a gift at the hotel! Rayne's thoughts raced as she tried to figure out why a stranger should leave gifts for her!

She thanked the receptionist and walked away from the desk, turning the unexpected present in her hands. She strolled into the lounge to wait for the taxi, feeling she should not go to her bedroom now that she had settled the account.

While she waited she tore open the paper and revealed the white box inside. She lifted the lid to reveal a facsimile doll of the one which she had given to Dean. They must clearly be an item made for the tourist market. She had noticed many such tiny figures dressed in Swiss national costume in the numerous shops stocking 'kitsch', but she had to admit that the one she held in her hands was a most charming example. It was more elaborate than those she had seen. The tiny features on the smiling face; the sparkling diamanté adornment on the blouse and full skirts; the doll was playing a tiny accordion which was also encrusted with diamanté stones, glittering as the sun caught them as she turned it in her hands. Every detail served to display the excellent workmanship. It was a real collector's item.

Rayne wished she had time to go back to the lakeside to return this gift to the stranger. She knew, though, that her taxi would be here at any minute. She did not wish to keep this memento of her stay—memories of this time were not happy. She sighed heavily. She seemed to have no alternative. Anyway— perhaps this souvenir would serve to remind her not to give her heart away too easily at some future date!

The arrival of her taxi distracted her from these reflections and, as they sped on their way to the railway station, Rayne's mind was too occupied by practical concerns to dwell on her problems. The station was busy and travellers' luggage, crammed with duty free purchases, overflowed on the platform around her. She was glad she had only one suitcase to worry about and felt a momentary sympathy for an elderly couple in front of her whose cases, bags and holdalls surrounded them like an encroaching sea around an island.

She did not have long to wait before the train's arrival. She had a corner seat and settled herself for the journey, an unopened paperback on her lap. She knew that the trite romance with its inevitable happy ending would only mock the reality which she had experienced recently.

As the train sped on its journey she gazed, unseeingly, out of the window. Tumbling mountain streams, cuckoo clock houses, white-capped mountains, verdant green meadows, bright wayside flowers all went unseen as the distance lengthened between Dean and herself.

She was aware only of the need to get home now; as if it were Shangri-La itself, the prospect of being once more in her small flat with her work to occupy her time offered her a refuge from the pain which racked her being. Dated commissions, which she had always conscientiously adhered to, would, at least, offer her a distraction from her preoccupation with Dean. There would be no time for bewailing a love that was not meant to be when she buckled down to serious work.

The hours passed. The book went unread. Her travelling companions chatted amongst themselves, but her obvious desire to concentrate on her own thoughts had communicated itself to them and they made no attempt to draw her into their conversation. The political situation and the fluctuating state of the business market made no impression on Rayne's engrossment with recent personal events.

Rayne never really remembered the formalities of arriving at Zurich *Bahnhof*, catching the airport bus and driving to Zurich airport. Mechanically she had done all that was necessary to get herself to her destination, but there was not one small detail which had penetrated her awareness.

It was only when she was actually fastening her seat-belt in the aircraft, preparing for take-off, that she recalled herself to the present and compared it with that previous journey when Dean had sat himself beside her. The memory was painful. She tried to thrust it away but the clear lines of Dean's features with those perceptive and unusual eyes continued to haunt her.

She tried to keep her attention fastened on the negative aspects of his character. He had clearly shown himself to be a philanderer and a no-good rake—and that was putting it lightly, she told herself. He had also shown that he was a criminal. Anybody who trafficked in drugs must surely lack all moral sense of duty to his fellow human-beings. She could not find one single exonerating circumstance to excuse his behaviour.

The seat beside Rayne was vacant

throughout the journey so there was no necessity for enforced exchanges with travelling companions. She was able to concentrate entirely upon the dark world of her own thoughts and conjectures. Of course she would never again see Dean Kenton. Not even Valerie would place her in a situation which necessitated a meeting between Dean and herself, she promised herself vehemently.

The flight passed without incident and Rayne was momentarily surprised when the announcement to fasten seat-belts was made. Lost within the speculations which bounded from Dean to Valerie and then back to herself, she had not noticed the swift passage of time. She felt a strange sense of sadness engulf her as she picked up her hand-baggage and started to alight from the plane. She felt a different person to the one who had set out so brief a time ago; then she had known the satisfaction of a well-organized life, pleasure in work efficiently done and an inner strength derived from her own positivity. Now she felt less able to cope with the traumas of living, almost reduced by her foolish love for so totally worthless a man.

Resolutely Rayne squared her shoulders, moving swiftly towards the green channel. She had nothing to declare. She was in no mood for purchasing even her duty-free quota of goods. All she wanted to do was to blank out the nightmare of the past days as if they had never been. If only she could wake up to find herself in her bed, a victim of a dream which had taken on all the horror of reality. But Rayne knew that none of this was a figment of imagination or self-delusion.

Not, that is to say, until she reached the airport concourse. Then she wanted to pinch herself to make sure she was really awake.

Standing in the middle of a group of strangers was Dean Kenton.

He saw her at the same moment her gaze had fallen on him. He was walking towards her. There was no doubt he had been waiting for her arrival on this flight.

CHAPTER SIXTEEN

Aghast, Rayne paused and stared at the man who approached her. Scarcely able to credit the evidence of her eyes, she was aware only that, as he towered over her, his lips were set in a hard, forbidding line; his expression was unreadable, unfathomable, but she felt herself tense in every nerve and muscle of her body as they came face to face.

Silence hung between them like a heavy curtain. Each was reluctant to be the first to speak as if it was a battle to test the strength of the other.

The bustle of the airport, teeming with activity, went on around them but Rayne was not aware of anything except this moment with its totally unexpected confrontation with the man who had occupied all her thoughts during the journey here.

'Hello, Rayne.'

His greeting broke the spell which surrounded them. Like a slow motion film gradually playing itself out before her eyes, she became alert to the life about them. Somewhere on the periphery of her consciousness she saw two other men closing in on Dean and herself. She moved aside, expecting them to pass. They made no attempt to do so but aligned themselves fractionally behind Dean's shoulder and within earshot. Their presence hampered Rayne, preventing her from demanding to know what Dean Kenton was doing here and why he had been awaiting her arrival on this flight. How, in heaven's name, had he even known that she was on it?

Her thoughts circled tempestuously as she felt a rising panic within herself. His expression remained grim and unsmiling; it was as if her own unfriendliness had communicated itself to him as he waited patiently for her to speak.

She swallowed hard, fighting down the increasing apprehension as she forced herself to acknowledge him. Her voice sounded breathy, nervous, unlike her own as she said:

'Dean! What are you doing here? How did you know I'd be on this flight . . .?—and—and who are these men?'

*   *

Sitting in the offices of the Secure Life Assurance Company an hour later Rayne was as bewildered as she had been at the airport. The cursory explanation she had received from one of the men accompanying Dean failed to provide her with any satisfactory answers to the questions she had posed during the journey here in the limousine which had been waiting outside for them.

She wanted to question Dean himself but, inexplicably, he seemed to have withdrawn himself from her. His manner was courteous but cold; there was no glimpse now of the laughing, teasing character who had dogged her footsteps during her sojourn in Switzerland. Where had he gone? Why was he hidden behind the grim façade of this steely-eyed stranger who sat behind the gigantic desk which separated them like an ocean?

'I'm sorry you've had to be brought here, Rayne,' he said at last. 'There are a few questions we have to ask though.'

'I do have a few of my own too,' she responded sharply. 'I wish you'd explain what's going on. I want to go home, Dean.'

His lips moved into a small smile without changing the hard expression in his eyes.

'I'm afraid we have to ask you to be patient

with us,' he said. 'It will all be clear to you later.'

Rayne sniffed disparagingly and shifted in the armchair, the movement signifying her annoyance with this unsatisfactory state of affairs. She knew that it would serve no purpose to argue, however, and allowed her gaze to rove the well-furnished office on the top floor of this building in the commercial heart of London. The entire décor was severe and plain. A few surrealist paintings were scattered about the cream walls, adding bright splashes of colour; numerous green plants and shrubbery were also on display; the thickly piled carpet was gold-toned and plain. Enormous double-glazed picture windows allowed no sounds of the busy traffic below to infiltrate into this atmosphere. She felt as if she were cut off from the rest of human society and wildly she found herself wondering if she would ever again be released from Dean's presence. Like a fast approaching tide she had the impression that events were shaping themselves about her and forming a constricting prison from which there could be no hope of escape.

She heard the sound of the door opening behind her and, glancing over her shoulder at the newcomer, she saw that it was one of the men who had been with Dean at the airport— the more senior looking of the two. He nodded curtly at her, handed a sheaf of papers to Dean and, without a word, sat himself down in the hard-seated chair over by the wall. His presence threw a stultifying blanket over Rayne but, turning away, she soon forgot he was there as she waited for Dean to speak.

'I believe you have a doll with you, Rayne,' he finally said. 'Where is it, please?'

'A *doll*. . . .?' Incredulously she stared at Dean, unable to believe her hearing. 'A *doll* . . .! Why should you be interested in a souvenir doll?'

'No ordinary doll this one, I assure you.' He smiled, again there was no real mirth in his expression. His tone hardened as he repeated: 'Where is it, please?'

'In—in my suitcase.'

As if waiting for an unobserved signal, the man who had been sitting on the sidelines, rose to his feet and left the room. Within a few moments he was back and Rayne saw he held her small case in his hands. He carried it to the desk and placed it on top in front of Dean before going back to his vacant chair.

'The key, please.' Dean stood up and held out his hand.

Rayne foraged in her handbag and passed the tiny silver key over to him. He unfastened the case, lifting back the soft top. Rayne was conscious of resentment at this intrusion into her belongings. The doll was on the top of her luggage. She remembered how she had used the task of putting it inside her suitcase in the train to Zurich as a pretext to surreptitiously wipe away her tears.

Dean Kenton lifted it out and then, as if still not entirely satisfied, he put the doll on the desk and flicked through the rest of the contents of the suitcase. Thank goodness that she had always taken a pride in the neatness of her packing, she thought, but this did not lessen the humiliation of prying fingers searching amongst her personal possessions. She glared indignantly at Dean.

'How dare you open my case!' she said. 'I would have given you the doll if that's what you're interested in.'

He glanced over at her, almost as if he had momentarily forgotten she was there and her angry response had recalled her presence to him.

'I just wanted to make sure you had only the one item,' he said.

'I could have told you that.'

'I would prefer you to tell me how this particular doll came into your possession.'

'It's a holidaymakers' souvenir. Easy enough for anybody to obtain surely?'

'Not quite like this example.' His eyes met hers levelly as he picked up the doll and scrutinized it carefully.

'But there's nothing wrong with it. It's the same as the one I gave you.'

He shook his head vehemently. 'No, Rayne, it isn't.'

'I know I had silly ideas about it being filled

140

with drugs but you agreed with me that the other was only a—an ordinary doll. This one is the same in every detail.'

'This one is worth nearly a million pounds to this company and I'm asking you to tell me exactly how it came into your hands.'

She blinked in disbelief. Slowly she started to tell him how she had returned to the hotel this morning to find the unexpected souvenir waiting for her. Out of the side of her eyes she detected an impatient shake of the head from the other man as if he did not believe her. She realized herself that her account sounded ineffectual and weak but she went on, trying to describe the elderly man who had accosted her at the lakeside. She told them that the receptionist's description of the man who had left the doll tallied with this stranger but her words sounded unconvincing even to herself.

Dean's expression was tolerant, bland; she thought she saw it soften as she stumbled and tripped over her words. She became conscious of the note of entreaty which was creeping into her tones. She fought against it, unwilling to allow Dean to catch even a glimpse of the perturbation which was rising within her.

'—and—and as it was the same as the other one that I'd made such a fuss about, I just—just put it in my suitcase and brought it home with me,' she finished her tale. Then: 'Are you telling me this one *does* contain drugs?' she added.

141

Dean shook his head, then picking up a pair of scissors from his desk, he carefully snipped away at all the diamanté stones which decorated the full skirts of the exquisitely dressed doll.

'Diamonds,' he said, with a smile. 'These stones are all real diamonds stuck on to the doll's clothing with a super adhesive.'

'*Real* diamonds?' Rayne gave the growing collection of stones on the desk in front of Dean a scathing glance. 'You must be mistaken. Nobody would do such a thing.'

'They would if they had been stolen in Holland and smuggled across to Switzerland en route for a diamond merchant in this country who is not too fussy about the origins of the gems he purchases.'

'But—I don't understand. The jewels would still be with me in London. What advantage would that be to—to whoever stole them?'

'Doubtless you would have had a burglary within a few days of your arrival home and the doll would have been "stolen". Don't forget, Valerie knows where you live.'

Rayne felt cold with disbelief. Then: 'Valerie? What has she to do with it? And where do *you* come into the affair?' she demanded sharply. 'I don't understand how you know so much about it.'

'I'm an insurance investigator, Rayne. It's my job to know about it. Your cousin got mixed up with a rather unsavoury crowd in Lugano

142

and information received anonymously led us to believe they were all involved in a plan to get the diamonds through customs—'

'Not Valerie. I don't believe you.'

Rayne felt herself swept along on a tidal wave of disbelief. Soon she would wake up from this nightmare and find she was back in her flat and none of this was true. But, somehow, even as she hoped for this, she felt her heart lowering within her as the words sunk in.

'She was only a pawn in their game. I believe she wasn't fully aware of the magnitude of the crime. She began to be frightened by the seriousness of what she'd got herself involved in as she learned more of their plans.'

'She believed that it was—was drug smuggling and told them—these people—' Rayne carefully made no mention that her cousin had mentioned Dean Kenton's name to her as being the chief malefactor—'she wanted nothing to do with it.'

'Possibly that's true. I'm afraid it didn't stop her sending for you to do her dirty work for her . . .'

'No . . .' Rayne felt suddenly faint but fought against the weakness. 'Oh, no . . .!'

Dean nodded. 'I'm afraid so . . . because of your strong resemblance to each other. She wanted them to believe she would be bringing the doll to England. She was afraid of repercussions if she refused to co-operate. She hit on the idea of getting you to act as the scapegoat for her while she hid out with friends.'

'How could she do such a thing to me!' Rayne didn't realize she had spoken aloud.

'Quite easily with the aid of an accomplice—'his eyes flashed with sudden anger—'who passed the doll on to you . . . and perhaps I find this the most distasteful part of the whole affair.'

'You seem to know so much,' Rayne murmured, 'but why do you assume I'm innocent?'

'I didn't at first. That was why I was keeping a very close eye on you.'

Rayne felt her heart lower. He never had been interested in her. Never! She concealed her thoughts and asked: 'When did you change your mind? What made you realize I knew nothing of what was going on?'

'As soon as you handed over the first doll to me . . . the one which had been hidden in your flower basket by Giovanni on my behalf. He is one of the company's employees and was working from the inside to keep watch on Francesco and his many friends. If you had been a party to the plot you would never have mentioned it to me at all.'

Rayne nodded her understanding, adding slowly: 'That was why you were so anxious I should give it to you . . . and also why you were watching the Hotel Bon Accord that night?'

'Yes.'

'And it was one of your men who searched my room while we were talking at the lakeside?' she hazarded a guess.

'Yes. He was checking to see if he could find any links with you and our criminal fraternity since you'd been hobnobbing with one of the heads of that particular crowd.'

'Francesco?' she asked.

'Yes,' he answered, with a smile.

'How did you know what you were looking for?' she asked next.

'A watch was being kept at all ports of entry for these diamonds. A replica doll had already been brought through customs decorated with gems. It was allowed to pass through as if undetected because we knew that the haul was incomplete. We guessed that they'd try the same method again since they believed it had worked so successfully.'

'I—I see.' She hesitated, suddenly anxious and almost fearing to ask her next question. But she knew the words must be spoken and, drawing in a deep breath, plunged into the matter which, at this moment, occupied all her attention. 'Valerie? What is to—to—' She broke off and tried again. 'What will happen to Valerie?'

'Very little. We—I shall try to keep her out of the affair as much as possible.'

Rayne felt her heart twist inside her. Of course he would protect Valerie. They were in

145

love with each other, weren't they? She felt the onrush of a pain she knew she must learn to accept.

'The main crooks have been rounded up and the diamonds are safely back and will be restored to their rightful owner as soon as possible. Our part in the matter is finished.'

He smiled kindly at Rayne and she felt the rise of tears to her eyes. She knew she was being foolish but, now that the mystery of the events had been brought out into the open she felt herself strangely drained and depressed. It was the anticlimax of it all, she told herself fiercely. It had nothing to do with Dean Kenton and her cousin. Nothing!

Suddenly she was filled with an urge to get out of this office. She wanted to get away from Dean and any reminder of the events which had caused her so many anguished hours. She needed to place distance between herself and this man. She hoped she would never meet him again. She rose to her feet almost as if in a numbed state of shock. Soon the pain would overwhelm her, would break all the restrictions she had placed upon it. She wanted to be alone when that moment arrived. The release that the threatening tears were offering was a temptation no longer to be denied.

She was already tired after her journey without this extra strain and she felt the weakness washing over her in wave after wave. She couldn't fight to control her emotions much longer and, with the knowledge, she stood up.

She stumbled and had to put out a hand to prevent herself from falling. Instead of touching the desk she found that Dean Kenton's arm was there to support her. She pulled her hand back as if the touch of his fingers had branded her.

He regarded her with sudden sharpness even as he turned and gave a dismissive nod of the head to the man who had been sitting in silent witness to their exchange.

He rose and departed from the room.

Rayne became instantly aware that the atmosphere in this office had thickened, charged with an undercurrent so intense that it almost seemed to paralyse her freedom to move.

Resolutely she took a step away from Dean, placing herself outside the reach of his grasp.

'May I go now?' She wondered if she had really spoken aloud as she intended; her voice no longer seemed to be in her control.

'You are in a great hurry to leave me, Rayne.' Dean spoke gently, almost teasingly. 'Is there nothing more we have to say to each other?'

'I think that far too much has already been said . . . and—and done . . . all in the interests of this insurance company,' she said coldly. 'You must save anything else you may have to say for Valerie. She may be gullible enough to

147

believe you. I am not.'

She turned away but, before she could take a step, Dean's hand had shot out to clutch her arm.

'Rayne! Don't be an idiot! I want to explain everything to you.'

'I already know all I want, thank you.'

She pulled her arm free from his grip and half-ran from the office. He called after her but she ignored him, intent only on making her escape. The tears were blinding her as she made her way to the street below.

It was like a nightmare sequence in a dream that the first person she should run into in the busy thoroughfare was Valerie herself.

A smiling Valerie. A Valerie who looked as though she had no problem in the world. Rayne felt a strong urge to take hold of her cousin and shake common sense into her.

'Rayne! What a bit of luck meeting you! I can see you've just been having the whole messy business explained to you.' She cast a glance at the tall buildings which housed the offices of the insurance company. 'I'm sorry I involved you in it. You've no idea the wrist-slapping I've had over it in there.' She nodded towards the doors behind Rayne.

'How *could* you have been so crazy as to get involved with such people as those in Switzerland?' Rayne struggled to keep her temper but her anger wanted to spill over in a flood of words. She fought to restrain them. To reveal the

148

true state of her feelings would be to spoil for ever the relationship which had once existed between them. Family ties were strong, forming a bond that even closest friendships could barely match.

Valerie had the grace to look penitent. She took Rayne's hand and clasped it for a moment before releasing it.

'Believe me, I *am* sorry, Rayne,' she said. 'I got in deeper than I meant to. I sent for you because I—I suppose I wanted to—to share my anxiety with somebody I trusted and loved.'

'Thanks a million!' Rayne spoke wryly. 'I'm surprised I'm not in jail because you trust and love me!'

'Please, try to understand.'

'I am trying but it's difficult to figure out how you could have been so stupid, Val.'

They were being jostled by the passers-by on the narrow pavement and Valerie, clutching Rayne's arm, drew her into the doorway of the building she had just left.

'Because I was in love, that's why!'

'Ah, yes. Dean Kenton. I almost forgot!'

Valerie gave a tinkling laugh which splintered like crystal in Rayne's ears.

'You will laugh when I tell you, Rayne, but—'

Rayne felt her head begin to whirl; even before Valerie spoke she knew intuitively that a moment of revelation had arrived.

'—the man who called himself Dean Kenton was actually using an assumed name because his boss—who actually *is* Dean Kenton—and he were trying to lay false trails to deceive the—the men who were trying to con me into bringing the diamonds through customs. While they were keeping their attention on my John Fairman the real Dean Kenton was busy following up various leads. Francesco, Marco and Barbara believed he was working for them. Isn't it all thrilling? . . . Just like a television series, don't you think . . .?'

Bemused by Valerie's voluble explanation, Rayne was still aware of the desolation which filled her heart. Perhaps if she had waited Dean himself would have explained why he had kissed her as he had. But did it matter? Clearly all he was concerned with was retrieving the wretched diamonds which had been the cause of so much worry and heartbreak for her.

Rayne felt herself nod at Valerie's childish prattle at the same time as she made a move to pass her cousin and leave the doorway of the building she hoped never to see again in her life.

'I must go home, Valerie,' she said. 'I'm tired after the journey from Switzerland. I haven't been home yet . . . I haven't eaten or—or anything.'

To her horror she felt a tear of self-pity slide down her cheek. She brushed it away swiftly, hoping that Valerie had not noticed. She need not have worried. Her cousin was too full of her own new-found happiness with the unknown John Fairman to observe Rayne's misery.

150

Even as Rayne made to leave Valerie, she saw her cousin's face light up with radiant joy. Following her gaze Rayne recognized the man as the stranger who had been sitting in Dean's office during their interview. This must, of course, be John Fairman. She did not need to stay and watch Valerie hurry to his side to know that. She ignored the plaintive request from her cousin to stay and be introduced to the newcomer. Enough was enough! Rayne told herself as she hurried along the street towards the taxi rank at the end.

It was only as she actually sat down in the taxi she realized that she had left her suitcase behind in Dean's office.

Nothing would make her go back to retrieve it. *Nothing!*

*   *   *

The walls of her flat pressed in on Rayne like a prison. She felt constricted both physically and spiritually by events, circumstances and emotions. Everything conspired to plunge her into the blackest depression she had ever experienced in her life. Fiercely, spiritedly, she fought the evil gremlins which weighed her down.

Free at last to indulge the luxury of tears she no longer wanted to shed them. Perversely she found that anger was dominant. She had been a pawn in a game and resented the fact that she

151

should have been manipulated by those around her.

The ring at the door-bell interrupted the tirade she was aiming at herself.

Valerie! she thought. She must have followed her here. Rayne's heart sank within her as she went to answer the door. She really did not feel like another session of romantic girl-talk and decided she would tell her she was just on her way out.

But it was not Valerie who stood on the other side of the door.

'Dean!' gasped Rayne, surprise taking her breath away for a moment. 'What on earth are you doing here?'

'What do you think? I've come to see you, of course ... and to return your suitcase to you. Didn't you realize you had left it behind?'

She nodded. 'I know.' Still she made no move to ask him inside.

'May I come in? I waited to see if you'd come back for this but you didn't.'

She stood back to let him pass and he stepped into the hall where he put down the suitcase. Wordlessly Rayne led the way into the living-room; once inside Dean seemed to tower over her and his very bulk made the room and furniture take on the dimensions of the miniature furniture in a doll's house.

He reached out a hand and, adroitly, she moved away. He let his hand fall to his side as if her snub had found its target. She told herself she was pleased but her heart denied it.

'Won't you sit down? Would you like a coffee?' she asked, covering her confusion by a formal show of politeness which was at odds with the tumult raging inside her.

He shook his head, curtly muttered 'Thank you' and sat down in the armchair. He looked uncomfortable. Rayne sat in a nearby seat and sought frantically for something to say. There should have been so much to discuss but, strangely, none of it seemed to be of any significance now. All the events which had taken place seemed to have happened in another lifetime far, far removed from this moment. The barrier between them seemed insurmountable now. Rayne wished he had not brought her suitcase back! What did a few personal items and clothing matter compared with the pain he was causing her by his very propinquity.

'Forgive me if I was rude to you in your office,' she began hesitantly. 'You must understand that it's all been rather a shock for me. I'm so sorry that my cousin became involved in the affair.'

'She's cleared now . . . and I gather that *some* good came out of it.'

'What do you mean?'

'Didn't she tell you? I looked out of the window and saw you talking to each other on the pavement outside the office. She's engaged to my assistant.'

Rayne nodded. 'Yes. She told me that.'

'John's a good man. He'll take care of her. Cheer up! She's not your responsibility any longer, Rayne.'

Rayne threw him a watery smile. 'No.'

'So why aren't you happy?'

'Of course I'm happy! I'm just—just—'

'Damned miserable?' Dean's mobile mouth twisted into a provocative smile.

'Why should I be miserable?' she demanded.

He made no effort to answer her rhetoric question and she added:

'I just feel as if I've been—*used*. By everybody.'

'Haven't you done your share of using people too?' he asked.

She stared at him dumbfounded before resentment stirred at the unfairness of his criticism.

'What are you talking about?' she demanded angrily. 'I've merely been a victim of circumstances.'

'Surely some good came out of it even for *you* too?'

'*Good*?' she echoed hollowly. 'I just want to forget everything about the last week. Forget all about everyone I met too.'

'So you didn't mean any of the kisses!' His voice was quiet, his tone expressionless; there was no question in the sentence but merely a statement of fact.

'No more than you did apparently,' she

154

retorted. 'I suppose it must all have been very amusing to you and a little flirtation must have helped to while away the boredom of the time for you.'

'I was hardly bored,' he said. 'Listen, Rayne, I have to tell you this whether you believe me or not, I—'

'I'm not interested in anything you have to tell me!'

'Too bad because I'm damn well going to do it—and what's more, you're going to listen.'

Swift as a rapier he stood up, thrust out his arm and, catching her by the wrist, pulled her from her chair, drawing her closer to him. She struggled to free herself but his grip only tightened the more until it was so painful she almost cried out. He gathered her into the circle of his arms and she could feel his breath stir through her hair even as she fought now against the onslaught of her emotions.

'I love you, Rayne. I always shall. Will you marry me?'

Suddenly she went limp within his arms. The nightmare had changed into a dream—and it was a dream from which she wished never to awaken.

'*Marry* you . . .?' she gasped.

He smiled. 'A quaint, old-fashioned little custom which means two people promise to love and care for each other until eternity! I'm all in favour of it. What about you, my love?'

Rayne's eyes were star-filled as she raised

her face to his.

'I'm in favour of it too,' she said. 'Just so long as it's *you* I can love.'

He uttered a small exclamation as his lips claimed hers in a sealing of the promise they had just made. The gentle kiss made a bond of their words.

Rayne felt again the surge of their shared passion as she gave herself freely into his embrace. This time there was no drawing back from the fulfilment of the joys which awaited them.

Are You Really Too Sensitive?

Are You Really Too Sensitive?

How to understand and develop
your sensitivity
as the strength it is

Marcy Calhoun

Intuitive Development Publishing

For information address:
Intuitive Development Publishing
1324 El Margarita Road
Yuba City, CA 95993
Orders: 530-755-4822

ISBN: 0-9677175-1-5

Library of Congress Catalog Number 87-7983

Library of Congress Cataloging-in-Publication Data

Calhoun, Marcy, 1940 -
    Are You Really Too Sensitive?

        1. Intuition (Psychology)   I. Title
BD311.C15   1987   133.8   87.7983
ISBN 0-9677175-1-5

Cover Illustration: Sharon Hartman

Printed in the United States of America by
Quebecor World Fairfield, Pennsylvania